P9-BYE-124

THE TEXAS TATTLER

All the news that's barely fit to print!

Fortunes Bestow Texas-Sized Welcome on Heirs!

Never let it be said that those Fortunes don't look out for their own. All of Red Rock is buzzing with news of the *ten-million-dollar* gift Miranda and Mary Ellen Fortune have bestowed on *each* of the "lost heirs." Local merchants are stockpiling electronics and "luxury goods"—just in case Miranda and Cameron Fortune's offspring want to unload some of that money.

Of course, it's not entirely clear that all of them need the money, especially Justin Bond. He's already made his mark in the steel industry and is one of Pennsylvania's leading businessmen. A source close to the Fortunes tells us that there *is* one thing this tycoon wants—his wife. Seems Justin and his college sweetheart have been estranged for the past year and during that time he became a daddy. Now, if you ask this reporter, that's an even bigger gift than *all the money* in Texas!

Dear Reader,

Welcome to the world of Silhouette Desire, where you can indulge yourself every month with romances that can only be described as passionate, powerful and provocative!

Silhouette's beloved author Annette Broadrick returns to Desire with a MAN OF THE MONTH who is *Hard To Forget*. Love rings true when former high school sweethearts reunite while both are on separate undercover missions to their hometown. Bestselling writer Cait London offers you *A Loving Man,* when a big-city businessman meets a country girl and learns the true meaning of love.

The Desire theme promotion THE BABY BANK, about sperm-bank client heroines who find love unexpectedly, returns with Amy J. Fetzer's *Having His Child*, part of her WIFE, INC. miniseries. The tantalizing Desire miniseries THE FORTUNES OF TEXAS: THE LOST HEIRS continues with *Baby of Fortune* by Shirley Rogers. In *Undercover Sultan,* the second book of Alexandra Sellers's SONS OF THE DESERT: THE SULTANS trilogy, a handsome prince is forced to go on the run with a sexy mystery woman—who may be the enemy. And Ashley Summers writes of a Texas tycoon who comes home to find a beautiful stranger living in his mansion in *Beauty in His Bedroom.*

This month see inside for details about our exciting new contest "Silhouette Makes You a Star." You'll feel like a star when you delve into all six fantasies created in Desire books this August!

Enjoy!

Joan Marlow Golan

Joan Marlow Golan
Senior Editor, Silhouette Desire

Please address questions and book requests to:
Silhouette Reader Service
U.S.: 3010 Walden Ave., P.O. Box 1325, Buffalo, NY 14269
Canadian: P.O. Box 609, Fort Erie, Ont. L2A 5X3

Baby of Fortune
SHIRLEY ROGERS

Silhouette®
Desire®

Published by Silhouette Books
America's Publisher of Contemporary Romance

Special thanks and acknowledgment are given to Shirley Rogers for her contribution to The Fortunes of Texas: The Lost Heirs series.

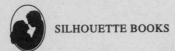 SILHOUETTE BOOKS

ISBN 0-373-76384-0

BABY OF FORTUNE

Copyright © 2001 by Harlequin Books S.A.

Visit Silhouette at www.eHarlequin.com

Printed in U.S.A.

Books by Shirley Rogers

Silhouette Desire

Cowboys, Babies and Shotgun Vows #1176
Conveniently His #1266
A Cowboy, a Bride & a Wedding Vow #1344
Baby of Fortune #1384

SHIRLEY ROGERS

lives in Virginia with her husband, two cats and an adorable Maltese named Blanca. She has two grown children, a son and a daughter. As a child, she was known for having a vivid imagination. It wasn't until she started reading romances that she realized her true destiny was writing them! Besides reading, she enjoys traveling and going to the movies.

Shirley loves to hear from readers. Please enclose a self-addressed, stamped envelope and write to: PMB#189, 1920-125 Centerville Tpke.,Virginia Beach, VA 23464.

THE FORTUNES OF TEXAS™

 Meet the Fortunes of Texas

Meet the Fortunes of Texas's Lost Heirs—membership in this Texas family has its privileges and its price. As the family gathers to welcome its newest members, it discovers a murderer in its midst...and passionate new romances that only a true-bred Texas love can bring!

CAST OF CHARACTERS

Justin Bond: This no-nonsense, hard-driven businessman has already made his mark in the world...but now he's realizing what matters most—family!

Heather Bond: Once she'd loved Justin with her whole heart, but a tragedy had ripped their marriage apart. Can she learn to love her husband again?

Timmy Bond: At three months, he is too young to understand how the events happening in this single month will shape his entire life....

Holly Douglas: Cameron's illegitimate daughter had refused to come to Red Rock...so now the Fortunes are taking matters into their own hands and heading to Alaska!

One

"Take your hands off my wife."

Justin Bond stood on the spacious porch of the home he'd once shared with his wife, and a flash of irritation whipped through him. He steeled himself to remain in control as he stared through the partially open door. He'd never expected to find Heather in the arms of another man.

Sucking in a hard breath, he balled his hands into fists at his side. His plans to woo his wife slammed into a brick wall. He'd come to ask her to give their marriage another try. It was a blow to his self-esteem to discover she was seeing someone else.

Reeling from the brutal tone of the warning, the man snapped his arms away from Heather, tripping over his own feet as he backed away. A nervous twitch appeared in his left eye. Justin considered that a victory of sorts.

"Justin!"

Shock and disbelief registered on his wife's face. She pressed a hand to her chest, as if unable to catch her breath. Or was she embarrassed to be caught in a compromising situation? Justin wasn't sure which, and at the moment, he didn't exactly care. He wanted this jerk out of his house.

"Heather." Justin swiftly shifted his gaze in her direction again, and annoyance swept through him like a sandstorm in the desert. He clenched, then relaxed his hands again.

"What are you doing here?" She didn't wait for him to answer as she looked from Justin to the other man, then back at her husband. Soft pink color stained her cheeks and neck, disappearing beneath the vee of her cream-colored blouse. "Um, you remember…uh, Paul…Paul Dailey, a colleague of mine from school?" Her voice trembled slightly.

Justin acknowledged the introduction with a slight nod. Twisting his lips, he studied his competitor. He hadn't thought much of Dailey when he'd first met him a few years ago at a school function with Heather. His blond hair was messy, his casual pants and shirt severely wrinkled. He'd always had that "slick salesman" look about him. Justin didn't trust him for a second.

It took every ounce of his willpower to restrain from storming into the room, grabbing the jerk by his collar and throwing him out of the house. Dammit! Heather was still *his* wife!

"Paul stopped by to discuss some…committee decisions we need to make."

Justin sent his wife a questioning glance. "Committee decisions?" His throat tightened as his gaze shifted with lightning speed to her companion. "Is that what you were *discussing* with my wife?" he asked pointedly. He put his hands on his hips, and it gave him a bit of pleasure to note a trace of fear in Dailey's eyes.

"We, uh, I...yes." Paul Dailey cleared his throat several times, and his hands flitted about nervously, as if disconnected from his arms. "Heather, we...uh, we can continue our discussion tomorrow at school." He snatched his briefcase from the floor and clutched it against his chest like a shield of armor. Without looking at her, he cautiously approached the door, his eyes watchful of the man challenging him.

Justin didn't move, forcing Dailey to squeeze his slender body through the small opening created between Justin and the doorjamb. Before Dailey was through the door, Justin reached out and flattened his hand against the jamb, preventing his escape.

"My wife is off-limits to anyone but me. In the future, you'd be smart to remember that." The threat of Justin's words was reinforced by his grave tone. He hesitated a moment, then dropped his arm. He heard the man's hurried footsteps, then a car door, and finally a revving engine and squealing tires. If he wasn't so irritated with his wife, he might have been amused.

As it was, Justin stared at the woman he'd married seven years ago, his heart slamming hard against the wall of his chest. Damn, just seeing her again after a year apart made his pulse race. Heather had always had that effect on him. She was still as beautiful as the day he'd met her on the campus of Penn State during his last year of school.

Watching him with uneasy eyes, Heather cau-

tiously stepped closer, stopping just in front of him.
She put her hand on the door, then leaned her hip
against it, hiking her short brown skirt higher on her
thighs. Her auburn hair fell in curls around her face
and shoulders. Black shoes with three-inch heels com-
plemented her shapely calves. Justin's muscles tightened as he remembered the last time he'd stroked her
legs, the last time they'd been intimate. His blood
pressure rose a notch.

Damn, a year was a long time without sex.

Apparently, it had been too long for Heather, also,
he thought, outrage pulling at him.

"That was uncalled for," she stated, her voice
sounding more stable as she began to absorb the
shock of seeing him. Small brackets formed a frown
around her full lips.

"Was it?" Justin shrugged one big shoulder. "The
wimp wanted to have you. I made sure he understood
he wouldn't."

He heard her intake of breath as her green eyes
darkened with emotion.

"You have no right to interfere with my life." Her
features tightened as she glared at him, a line between
her eyes becoming prominent.

"You're still my wife," Justin reminded her. "Apparently you've forgotten that."

"I haven't forgotten that we're still married." She
faced him squarely, her shoulders visibly tightening.
"But I easily could have. I haven't heard a word from
you in a year." The reminder was spoken sharply,
and hurt lingered in the shadows of her eyes. After
she'd miscarried their baby, Justin had withdrawn
from her. Eventually their marriage had suffered ir-
reversible damage, and he'd chosen to leave her. The

pain of his rejection still had the power to make her heart ache.

Justin stated the obvious. "I'm here now. May I come in?"

As she stared at her husband, Heather's whole carriage stiffened. Her heart tripped over itself as his gaze held hers captive. He was so handsome that he literally stole her breath. Impeccably dressed in a white shirt and dark business suit, he looked as if he'd come straight from work. Justin always had a presence about him, something about him that commanded attention wherever he was, whoever he was with.

She glanced back up at his face. His well-groomed dark brown hair was combed back from his face, and his blue eyes were blatantly perceptive as they studied her. Though she could never quite read what Justin was thinking, she wished now, more than ever, that she had such power.

What was he doing here? Could it be that he still loved her? Flushing at the foolish thought, she dismissed it. She'd given up that hope long ago. Besides, she wasn't going to let him hurt her again. There was no way in hell she could stand the torture of losing him again.

"I don't think that's a good idea," she told him, then frantically glanced behind her and into the living room, praying that none of her baby's things were visible. It was the one area of the house that she tried very hard to keep straight.

A flash of guilt swept through her, temporarily paralyzing her. She'd never told him that when he'd walked away from her, he'd left her pregnant. He had no idea that he had a three-month-old son. Knowing

Justin, if she'd told him, he would have felt obligated to come back to her—and Heather hadn't wanted him back on those terms. A child wasn't a good reason to keep a marriage together. She'd learned that cold hard fact when her own father had deserted her and her mother when she was thirteen.

Her husband's unexpected arrival on her doorstep unnerved her. Was it possible he'd learned of Timmy's existence? Panic seized her—the hard, gripping kind that twisted and tortured every muscle in her chest.

"I'd like to talk to you." Justin spoke with obvious control. Though he appeared calm, the underlying determination in his tone spoke volumes.

Heather glanced at her watch and realized she was very late picking up Timmy. Nerves made her stomach tighten as she weighed the consequences of allowing Justin inside. She was thankful she'd had a few errands to run after school, and hadn't swung by her mother's for her baby.

"Maybe some other time," she suggested coolly, dropping her hands to her side. Dispassionately, she continued, "I have another appointment in a few minutes." It was the wrong thing to say.

Justin stared directly at her, his curiosity apparently piqued. "What kind of appointment?"

"Just something I need to take care of," she offered vaguely. She combed her hair away from her face with her fingers. "Look, can't this wait?"

"It'll only take a few minutes," he insisted, stepping closer. "What harm could there be in inviting me in?"

His words made her skin burn hot, and Heather immediately assured herself that her reaction was only from seeing him so unexpectedly, not at all because of his nearness or the familiar scent of him. No, she couldn't afford to let her heart respond to him.

"None, I assure you," she retorted, then wished she hadn't let him provoke her.

"Then let me in—" his lips curved ever so slightly "—since you have nothing to be afraid of."

Heather thought about it for a moment. Well, technically he *was* still her husband, even if she didn't want to acknowledge that fact to him. That they'd been separated for a year apparently meant nothing at all to him. And she really couldn't refuse, since he still owned the house they'd shared through six years of marriage.

She shifted and moved away from the door. "All right. For a few minutes."

Justin stepped inside, and then he shut the door behind him. As he entered the foyer and then the living room, his gaze slowly swept it, as if cataloging every item in minute detail.

His scrutiny made Heather edgy, and she glanced about, again searching the room to be sure it was free of anything that belonged to her son. Then she walked over to the sofa and stopped beside it. "Would you like to sit down?" She gestured toward the chair across from her.

"I'll stand." Justin walked farther into the room.

His gaze swept her from head to toe, and she nervously smoothed her hair with her hand. The curls refused to cooperate, and she tucked a stray strand behind her ear.

"How long have you been seeing Dailey?" It came out sounding like a blunt demand.

"We're just friends. I haven't been *seeing* him."

Justin stared at her, his expression disbelieving. "Then that was the first time he's come on to you?"

Heather blushed furiously.

"I didn't think so."

"All right, I'll admit that it wasn't, but that doesn't mean anything!" She put her hands on her hips to stop them from shaking. He had the power to annoy her without even trying. Apparently he hadn't changed. Justin always had to be in control. It was one of the things she'd first admired about him. He'd been a no-nonsense, hard-driven, dependable person in her life when she'd needed someone to care for her. After years of struggling with feelings of abandonment by her father, it had been easy for her to let him take charge.

But she was no longer the love-starved young girl he'd married. She no longer needed someone to lean on, someone to protect her and take care of her.

"I see."

"Apparently you don't," Heather retorted, taking in his skeptical expression. "Maybe Paul's asked me out a few times, but I've always refused." Heather had her hands full working full-time as a teacher and being a mother.

Okay, so maybe she got lonely once in a while, but she wasn't ready to date again. She didn't have time for a relationship, nor did she want one. She knew too well how easy it was to get hurt.

Justin's jaw tightened a fraction. "He didn't look as if he was going to take no for an answer just now," he remarked.

"*You* didn't give me a chance to make it clear to him that I wasn't interested."

"If he's come on to you before and you've discouraged him, apparently he isn't getting the message," he reasoned, and a muscle worked in his jaw.

Heather gave a frustrated sigh. "I really don't see that this is any of your business. You've been out of my life a long time, Justin, and I don't owe you any explanations."

He favored her with a curious look, lifting his brow in question. "We're still married."

She bristled, annoyed by the intimate reminder she saw in his eyes. "We haven't lived together in a year," she stated, resolving to end the conversation.

"That's why I came to see you."

Heather paled and her breath caught. She felt as if she'd been punched in the chest.

He's come to ask you for a divorce!

She trembled before she brought herself under control. Though totally unprepared for this, she could handle it. She could, dammit! Shaking her head, she realized she should have expected that he'd find someone new.

"You want a divorce," she stated flatly, denying him the chance to tell her he was in love with someone else.

A small smile gradually spread on Justin's lips, just enough to expose a trace of the dimple in his right cheek. Heather's heart hammered. His smile was what had first attracted her to him. His smile and that damn attractive dimple.

"What?" Confusion etched her brow. Feeling lightheaded, she touched the back of the sofa for support. "Isn't that why you're here?"

"No."

She glanced at his hand, and for the first time realized he still wore his diamond-and-gold wedding band. "Why *are* you here, then?"

Justin regarded her silently, then seemed to choose his words very carefully. "Actually, I want us to give our marriage another try, Heather."

"What?" Heather couldn't have heard him right. Surely, her mind was playing tricks on her.

"You heard me correctly," he assured her, apparently reading the bewilderment on her face. "I want us to give our marriage another chance." He stepped closer to her, and she immediately took two steps away from him.

"I don't understand," she whispered softly. This didn't sound at all like the Justin who had turned his back on her and walked out on their life together after her miscarriage. "I mean, why?" She wondered again if he knew about Timmy. But from the way the conversation was going, that was doubtful.

Justin reached toward her and touched his fingers to her cheek. She moved her head a fraction, out of his reach, and he let his hand fall. "A lot has happened in the year we've been apart. "

"Such as?" she prompted. What could possibly have happened that would have a bearing on their marriage? she wondered suspiciously.

He'd never been one to open up, and she'd always thought they would have had a chance if he'd told her what he was thinking, what he was going through.

"I met my birth mother."

She blinked with surprise. "You have? Really?"

Heather was stunned that he was talking about his past. She always believed the reason that Justin was so reserved and reluctant to share his feelings was the way he was raised. As a baby, he'd been left on the doorstep of a sheriff's office in Nevada. Because he was unable to be put up for adoption, he'd been placed with a foster family, had been given their last name. He'd grown up in the foster-care system, had been shuffled around all his life. He was never allowed to put down roots, never given the opportunity to become part of a family.

When they'd first married, she'd thought that they would put down their own roots. Naively, she had believed they'd be together forever. She couldn't have been more wrong.

Justin gave her a slight nod. He hesitated a moment, then continued, "Her name is Miranda Fortune and she lives in Texas."

Heather wasn't sure what to say. Justin seemed…somehow pleased by this new development in his life. "Oh, Justin." She sighed, and her heart swelled with caring. Despite the heartache he'd caused her, she was happy for him.

Justin had been searching for something all his life, something to fulfill him. He seemed to have found it. The realization that it wasn't her, that she hadn't been enough to make him happy, stung, even as her compassion for him flourished.

"How did you find her?"

"I didn't." He shoved his hands in his pockets. "Her ex-husband, Lloyd, sent a private detective to look for me. The P.I.—Flynn Sinclair—eventually contacted me and asked me to go to Texas to see her."

"And you did?"

He nodded. "At first I refused. Then I learned that I have a twin, a sister." Justin could understand Heather's surprise at his news. He'd felt the same overwhelming disbelief when the detective had shown up at his office to tell him of his heritage. His first reaction had been indifference. His mother hadn't cared enough to keep him—why should he give her the satisfaction of knowing him now?

But learning he had a twin had convinced him to change his mind. There was another part of him somewhere in the world, someone with some of the same personality traits, the same looks, the same feelings of abandonment and emptiness. Based on that, he'd agreed to a meeting.

"A twin sister?"

The thought of his sister brought a smile to Justin's lips. He touched the dimple on his cheek and remembered his surprise when he'd first seen that she, too, shared the identical physical trait. "Her name is Emma," he said to his wife. "She's just had a baby, and she ended up marrying Flynn Sinclair." Seeing the confusion on her face, he added, "It's a long story."

"My goodness." She sounded as if she couldn't believe it. "A lot *has* been happening. I'm very pleased for you," she said. "What is your mother like?"

"She seems nice, and is interested in learning more about me," he explained, his tone noncommittal. "Miranda was very young when she had us, and on her own. She felt that there was no way she could take care of us. Later, she married and had two other children—so I have two other siblings, as well.

"I've seen them all on a few occasions," Justin continued. "The first time was several months ago when I first went to Texas to meet Miranda and Emma. I saw Miranda again just a few days ago at a party given by my half-brother, Kane and his wife Allison, welcoming me into the Fortune family.'' Justin had even considered moving to Texas, but had quickly realized that leaving Pittsburgh would add a finality to his relationship with Heather. He wasn't prepared to do that. Not yet.

"You have a brother?"

Justin nodded. "Yes. He's a doctor and he also lives in Texas. So does my half-sister, Gabrielle, who is married to the town sheriff and has a daughter.''

"And you've already met them all?'' Heather could imagine Justin's manner as he met the strangers who were related to him. Even as he spoke of them now, she could see the reservation in his eyes. That he'd called his mother by her first name revealed more than he intended. He'd met these people—relatives—but he wasn't yet willing to call them family.

"As I said, several times.'' He moved across the room and picked up a framed picture on a drop-leaf table. It was of the two of them on their wedding day. Deep in thought, he rubbed his thumb over the picture.

Heather wished at that moment that she'd put it away. She didn't want him to think it meant something to her. She'd kept it out to remind herself of the mistake she'd made by believing he truly loved her.

"Apparently the Fortunes are obscenely wealthy,'' Justin stated, sounding notably unimpressed as he studied the smile on Heather's face in the picture. Their wealth hadn't been what had encouraged him to meet Miranda or the Fortunes. At eighteen, he'd moved to Pittsburgh with the last foster family he'd lived with. A short time later, when they'd moved again, he'd moved out on his own. He'd worked two jobs and attended college.

He'd made a place for himself in the world— owned his own prosperous steel business, Trigon Steel, which earned enough money for him to live on quite comfortably for the rest of his natural life even if he never worked another day.

But it wasn't enough to fill the void inside him, and what actually prompted him to meet his biological mother was her connection to his own existence. It was finally knowing where he'd come from, who he was linked to in the world, that had taken him to Texas.

"Your mother never searched for you before?"

"I don't think so. When Miranda was young, she never wanted any affinity with the Fortune family, but she's since made peace with them. She wants Emma and me to be a part of the family, too."

"What about your biological father? Have you met him as well?"

"No, we haven't discussed who my father was." Though he was curious, he hadn't asked.

He looked at Heather and saw confusion clouding her green eyes. She couldn't imagine why meeting his family had provoked this visit from him, nor did she have any idea why he thought they should make another go of their marriage. How could he make her understand, when he wasn't quite sure he understood himself?

Seeing all of the Fortune family together had made an impact on his hardened heart. Through troubles and tribulations, they'd stuck together, found offspring they didn't know existed and brought them under the umbrella of their family. They'd supported each other, had opened their arms to welcome him and Emma.

"And what exactly does all of this have to do with me?" Heather finally asked, after listening to his explanation. "With us?"

"Miranda would like to meet you."

"But, why?"

"Because you're my wife."

Justin's answer was too simple to make sense. Heather couldn't imagine why his biological mother would want to meet her, especially since she and Justin were separated.

When she didn't reply, he swung around to face her. She felt the full force of his heated gaze as it traveled very slowly over her body, then rose with meticulous precision to her face. Butterflies attacked her stomach. She had an eerie feeling she wasn't going to like what he was going to say.

"I'd like you to go to Texas with me."

Two

"To Texas?" Heather's voice rose a pitch as she stared blankly at her estranged husband. He couldn't really mean what he was suggesting.

He frowned deeply at her reaction. "That *is* where she lives." There was the briefest hint of frustration in his tone. "I'd like you to meet her, as well."

Heather's mouth was still hanging open. "You would?" Knowing her husband wasn't prone to spontaneous actions, she figured there had to be more to this. For someone like Justin, who needed to control everyone and everything around him, well, she figured, adjusting to his new family had to be very hard for him to deal with.

She was certainly curious about the Fortunes. Apparently they'd made quite an impression on him. He seemed so...she couldn't really put her thoughts into words. Justin was somehow undefinably...different.

"Of course."

"Why didn't you just tell your mother we were separated?"

He hesitated, then said, "Because I thought maybe you and I still had a chance together. There's no reason for her to know otherwise, if we stay together." He moved a step closer to her. "It's not so crazy when you think about it. We were happy once, Heather." He reached toward her and ran his fingers across her cheek, then through her hair to brush it from her face.

She stiffened, again moving a step away. "I thought we were," she agreed, "until..." She left the words unspoken, but the reminder was there all the same. Heather's skin tingled where he'd touched her, and she suspected he wasn't just talking about their marriage. For a while, they had shared something special, and she had no trouble remembering those wonderfully happy times. Those memories taunted her often, as did the memory of the moment he'd left her.

"We both made mistakes, but we had a good life for a while."

"I haven't forgotten, Justin." Her admission came reluctantly, and brought a barely noticeable look of relief to his features.

"Maybe we can recapture what we had."

"Justin—"

"We were married for six years," he interrupted, his tone slightly challenging. "Doesn't that mean anything to you?"

She bristled. "I could ask you the same thing. I haven't heard a word from you in a year, and now you show up wanting me to go away with you."

"You didn't bother to contact me, either," he reminded her sharply.

Heather felt a wave of embarrassment sweep over her. His charge was justified, more so than hers. She'd had more reason to contact him than he knew. "You're right, but—"

"Come to Texas with me," he said again, softening his tone. He cocked his head and studied her. "That's all I'm asking. It'll give us time to think about what's happened between us, time to decide where we should go from here." Surprise filled her gaze once again. "Would you be willing to try again to make our marriage work?"

"I...I don't know," she answered honestly, astonished at how her pulse raced at the thought. Could she really risk her heart again?

Justin didn't say anything for a moment. He turned and went to the window and stared out of it. Heather nervously bit her bottom lip, wondering what he was thinking. Just as she was about to speak, he turned and faced her.

"How about if we give it a month?" He walked back over to her and stopped so close that she could feel his body heat. "One month. Isn't our marriage worth a month out of your life?"

Heather swayed, staggered by his proposition. "A month," she repeated. He was putting a timetable on their reconciliation. Now, that sounded more like the Justin she remembered. Always in control.

Justin nodded. "It's long enough to see if we can work things out," he rationalized. "If after a month it isn't working, I'll give you a divorce." His jaw tightened a fraction.

Heather still couldn't believe this was happening,

and she was hesitant to give him the power to hurt her again. Yes, she still had feelings for her husband—but only because he was the father of her son. And what about when he learned about their baby? Would Justin use Timmy to pressure her into staying married?

She was astute enough to realize that she saw very little change in Justin. He was still a man of few words, still kept his thoughts to himself. Though Heather had always felt during her marriage that he cared for her, he had never really said the words. She supposed she couldn't blame him. Words of love never came easy to her, either, and she'd held back her own thoughts and feelings. It was also obvious that he still wanted to control everything around him.

However, in the past year she'd changed, grown independent. She was used to making decisions for herself.

Deep in thought, Heather was unaware of how close Justin had come to her until he reached for her and drew her against him. Caught by surprise, she put her hands flat against his hard-muscled chest. In the past, they'd settled many problems in each other's arms—the last being when she'd gotten pregnant with Timmy. But she wasn't going to let him get away with it now.

Not this time.

Leaning backward, she put enough pressure in her arms to break his embrace. He frowned, and his lips flattened into a thin line. But he let her go. She stepped farther away, enough to feel as if she could breathe normally again. She hated the way he had of stealing her breath with his mere presence.

"One month, Heather."

The ringing of the telephone startled them both. Heather murmured an apology. "I have to get that," she said, suspecting it was her mother. Quickly moving across the room, she picked up the telephone receiver on the end table.

"Hello," she said. "Oh, Mom. Yes, I know I'm late. I'm sorry." She glanced at Justin before quickly looking away.

He watched her talk on the phone with her mother. He'd always liked Kathryn Watson. She was warm and attentive without being controlling or smothering—the kind of mother that he'd always yearned for, the kind of mother he'd never known. Now that he'd met Miranda, Justin thought she, too, seemed to be kindhearted and caring. She'd made an effort to get close to him, but so far he hadn't been able to totally let his guard down around her—or any of the other Fortunes.

His reserve around his extended family didn't include his sister Emma. He and his twin shared a certain respect for each other, a bond that only twins could feel. He'd been amazed by her easygoing nature, despite her troubled past. When they'd met, he'd learned she was on the run from an abusive exboyfriend. Had he not been reassured by Sinclair that Emma would be safe with him, Justin would have taken care of her himself. The thought of someone hurting her infuriated him. Justin was pleased that Emma had found Flynn, who loved her and her newborn daughter.

"I have some unexpected company."

Heather's voice drew his attention, and he wondered what Kathryn would say if she knew it was him. He strained forward to hear what he could of the conversation, and it was obvious she was avoiding telling her mother about him. Well, that was okay. Kathryn would know soon enough that he wanted to reconcile.

His wife sighed heavily. "It's Justin, Mom." She listened for a moment. "I'm going to be a few minutes longer, if that's okay." More silence, and her foot tapped the floor nervously. "Thanks, Mom. I really appreciate it."

Heather hung up the telephone, then turned to face him. Her expression was shadowed, probably out of a need for self-preservation. But Justin didn't miss the brief glimpse of awareness in her eyes, and he took that as a sign that she still felt *something* for him.

She ran the pink tip of her tongue over her upper lip, and he bit back an oath. He wanted nothing more at that moment than to pull her to him and make love to her, to show her there was an underlying spark between them that they could build on.

She represented everything he'd worked for in his life—and everything he'd been unable to hold on to. He'd lost the woman he'd loved, his home, and with her unfortunate miscarriage, the family he'd wanted so badly. They'd had a chance once. Was it irrational to believe they could have another?

He resisted the urge to pull her back into his embrace, and as though she needed to put space between them, she stepped farther away from him and stood beside one of the big overstuffed chairs that decorated the room.

Her hands tightened on the back of the chair, her knuckles turning white. She looked...wary, and Justin could understand that. He'd deeply disappointed her once, although he'd thought he was doing the right thing by giving her her freedom. It was going to be hard for her to put those unpleasant memories to rest and consider his proposal.

She held her head high and looked him directly in the eyes. ''This is so like you,'' she commented. ''I mean, showing up so suddenly, making decisions and expecting me to agree to whatever you want.''

Annoyed by her words, Justin grimaced. ''I called and left you a message, letting you know that I'd be coming over.''

Heather's gaze swung to the answering machine sitting on the table. The little red message light was blinking. ''I haven't had time to check my messages. As soon as I came in the door, Paul arrived.''

''Would it have made a difference if you'd known I was coming?''

''I don't know.'' She searched his face, wishing for even a hint as to what he was thinking. ''We didn't exactly part on good terms.'' Truthfully, they hadn't exactly parted on *any* particular terms. He had simply walked away from her one day.

Later, he'd contacted her through his lawyer, who had informed her he would be sending her a monthly check. Once she'd realized that he wasn't coming back, she slowly started putting her life back together.

Then she'd discovered she was pregnant again.

They'd made love one of the last evenings they'd spent together. On her part, it had been a desperate attempt to regain some closeness between them. Heather hadn't taken precautions, and neither had Justin. Even up to the very end, she'd hoped to have another child. She had foolishly thought another baby would help her marriage, had hoped Justin would love her if she gave him a child.

But he'd left, anyway. It wasn't long afterward that

she had started missing her periods. When she'd found out she was pregnant, she was elated, yet deeply saddened by the irony of her situation. She realized she was going to have the baby they'd always wanted—only Justin wouldn't be there to share the joy with her.

She'd hoped he'd contact her, give her some idea he still cared for her. But he hadn't, and she had decided at that point not to tell him about her pregnancy. She'd thought about it long and hard. But dealing with his rejection had been so difficult, and she'd known he would have come back to her only because of the baby. Heather just couldn't live with him knowing that her love wasn't enough to make him happy.

For a while, she'd been worried he'd find out somehow, or that their paths would cross and he'd discover the truth. Fortunately, Pittsburgh was a very big city. Justin's office was across town in the Pittsburgh Plate Glass building, and their house in the elite suburb of Fox Chapel was far enough away that she'd hoped her secret was safe. Apparently she hadn't had to worry about it. Justin had never even tried to see her—until now, and the friends they'd had had dropped out of her life when she no longer traveled in the same circles.

Justin's lips curved into the bare resemblance of a smile. She hadn't seemed surprised when he'd shown up. "My intent in coming here wasn't to run rough-shod over you." His gaze was direct. "My motives aren't suspect. I'm *asking* you to give us another chance."

When she didn't answer right away, he felt his heart stop. His plans for a reconciliation depended on getting Heather alone with him so he could convince her to give their marriage another try.

"I don't know. I need to think about this," she stated frankly.

Though he didn't necessarily like her answer, he decided not to pressure her. He'd give her some time to think about it, then see where that got him. He had a tenacious nature and wasn't one to give up easily if something was important to him.

That had a lot to do with his past. It hadn't been easy getting past abandonment and growing up in foster care. Justin had never been fortunate enough to live with a family who cared about him.

He hadn't stayed with any one family very long. There had always been a reason to get rid of him, no matter how hard he'd tried to fit in. He'd been too young or too old, too reserved or too much trouble. At a very early age he'd learned to look out for himself.

He should thank Miranda for instilling in him a drive to make something of himself. In a perverse way, her abandoning him as a baby had implanted the motivation to become independent and successful.

"All right." He stared at her a moment, then reached for her hand. He was both surprised and pleased when he realized she still wore his ring. He touched it, then watched the large, tear-shaped diamond sparkle in the light from the window. She drew her hand away, and he frowned. "I'll call you tomorrow."

Heather pressed her lips together as she followed him to the door. "No," she said quickly, wanting to control their next meeting. "I have school and a meeting afterward. I'll call you. Where will you be?"

Reaching inside his jacket, he extracted a business card. "You know the office number. This has the number of my apartment, as well as my digital."

Heather studied the card as he opened the door. "All right, I'll call you after school tomorrow."

Justin nodded, then stepped outside. He hesitated, then turned back toward her. "I'll see you tomorrow."

Heather watched him get into his Mercedes and drive away. As he disappeared from sight, she sagged against the door, her strength zapped.

Justin's visit had blindsided her. Even a tornado wouldn't have caused such havoc in her life.

Was she losing her mind? She'd actually told him she'd think about his proposition—that she'd consider giving their marriage another try.

Did she really want to?

A long time ago she'd loved Justin. Could she learn to love him again?

Three

―――

"**H**ow did he look?" Kathryn Watson asked as soon as they had settled around the kitchen table to eat dinner.

"Justin?" Heather asked needlessly. "The same. Too handsome for his own good." She twirled a few strings of spaghetti around on her fork, then took a bite and chewed thoughtfully. There wasn't a woman on earth who wouldn't look twice at him if she passed him on the street.

"Does he know about Timmy?"

"No! Oh, my, Mom. That's what I thought, too, when I saw him." She explained that she'd stopped off at home for a few minutes to bring some things into the house and that Paul Dailey had shown up. Heather also told her of the altercation between her husband and Paul.

Kathryn chuckled, and Heather shot her mother a glare. "It wasn't funny."

"I wish I'd been there," Kathryn said. "Justin's always been very protective of you. I bet he was seething."

"He was overbearing and rude," Heather retorted, taking another bite of her food.

"Well, at least that problem's solved. You've been discouraging him for months."

"Yes, well, Justin didn't have to be so...blunt," she said, for lack of a better word.

"Funny, that's one of his traits that I've always admired. Justin's not a man of many words, but when he says something, he's direct. What did he want?" she asked.

Heather told her about Justin's heritage and how he'd gone to Texas to meet his biological mother and twin sister.

"Well, I couldn't be happier for him. He's always been so alone in the world, without family, growing up being passed from foster home to foster home."

Kathryn had always told Heather that she found Justin's drive to be one of his greatest strengths. He'd majored in business, and after graduation he'd worked for a while in the steel industry, then started his own steel fabrication company. Trigon Steel was now a major player in a city where the competition was stiff and often brutal.

"He had me. I was his family," she reminded her mother, her eyes cloaked with sadness. "He walked away from what we had."

"He was hurting, as you were. Justin isn't anything like your father, honey. Henry was manipulative and selfish. He never led me to believe there was anything wrong between us. If I'd known he was having an affair, I would have left him long before he left us.''

"Dad didn't care about you or me.'' Heather's eyes glistened, and she looked away.

She had a tremendous amount of respect for her mother. Kathryn Watson was strong and independent. She'd raised her daughter alone, had worked overtime hours as a secretary to help her pay for college. Heather was fortunate to have her mother as her best friend and confidante.

However, her father's desertion remained with her throughout her life. Though her mother had dealt with his betrayal, Heather was never able to express the hurt and rejection that was always a part of her.

Kathryn remained silent for a moment, then said quietly, "Not all men leave.''

"Justin did.'' Heather couldn't forget that. His leaving had effectively reinforced the wall around her heart.

Kathryn reached across the kitchen table and touched her daughter's hand. "Everyone handles grief differently. Justin handled it the only way he knew. He threw himself into his work. He didn't know how to relate what he was feeling.''

"Mom, you've always championed Justin.'' She wrinkled her brow, deepening her frown. "I know you've supported me, too, but why is it you feel the need to come to his defense?''

"Because he's never had anyone to do that for him,'' Kathryn answered softly. "I can't imagine what it must be like to grow up without any connection to the world. No family, no distant relatives, no one.''

"Well, now he has an entire family, complete with

a half brother and sister. Apparently, they're extremely rich.'' She shoved her plate away and sat back in the chair. ''Mom, he wants me to go to Texas to meet his mother and he has this…this weird idea of us giving ourselves a month together to see if we can work things out between us.''

Speechless, Kathryn stared blankly at her daughter. ''A month? What did you tell him?''

''That I needed to think about it. What else could I say?'' Gauging her mother's thoughtful expression, Heather asked, ''What do you think?''

''Marriages aren't always easy, honey. The fact that Justin has come to you means a lot. He must still have feelings for you. And how would you feel if you gave up this chance? You have Timmy to think about, as well as yourself. You're going to have to tell him about Timmy, Heather.''

Heather saw the censure in her mother's eyes. ''I know. And I will. Just not yet.'' She flushed as guilt ate at her. She *had* intended to tell Justin about the baby before now, really she had. It was ironic that he'd shown up and had effectively taken away her chance to come clean voluntarily. ''I know Justin, and if he found out about his son, he'd insist on reconciling for that reason alone. I don't want a marriage based on sacrifice.''

Kathryn picked up Heather's plate and took it to the sink. ''Look, why don't you think about going to Texas? You'll be alone together, and it will be the perfect opportunity to see if you can salvage your marriage.''

''I can't just up and run off to Texas, Mom. I have responsibilities here. I have Timmy to take care of.''

''Don't use Timmy as an excuse,'' Kathryn

scolded. "I can keep him for you, and you know he'll be safe with me."

Heat darkened Heather's already flushed face. Her mother wasn't easily fooled. Using Timmy *was* a quick and easy excuse she could hide behind. "All right, I know that."

"Then go home and think long and hard about what Justin has proposed."

Later at home, Heather could think of nothing else. Did she dare do as her mother encouraged? She wasn't even sure if she could leave Timmy for a long period of time. He was so little, and he needed her. Since his birth, she hadn't been away from him, other than the hours she was at school. How could she abandon him to her mother for a month?

There was no way she could leave Timmy. She'd just have to think of something else, she decided, her head full of decisions to make, her heart heavy.

"Your wife is on line four."

"Thank you, Ms. Harris," Justin responded, and realized his voice wasn't as steady as he'd have liked.

He'd been impatiently waiting for Heather to call, had instructed his secretary to put her through immediately. He'd even picked up the telephone several times to call her, only to put it back down. Aware his hands were sweating, he rubbed them on his slacks, then picked up the receiver and punched a button on the telephone.

"Heather?" He was anxious to hear her husky voice, to hear her say his name. Her effect on him even after one short visit was lethal. She was all he could think about.

"Hi. Is this a bad time?"

Justin thought she sounded a little rattled. Well, he could relate to that. His uncertainty as to what she was thinking or what her decision might be had made him irritable. His secretary had threatened to quit after working with him for only a few hours this morning. He knew the reason, and its name was Heather.

"No, of course not. You can call me anytime."

"Oh." There was silence on the line while she digested that. "Well, I'll only keep you for a moment. I was wondering if we could meet. You know, to talk."

"Of course," he assured her, enjoying the breathless sound of her voice as she spoke. It wrapped around him, warming him like a blanket on a cold, snowy day. "How about if I stop by the house this evening?" he suggested, wanting to see her again as soon as he could. He'd drive there right now if she said the word.

"No," she replied quickly. "I, um, have some business to attend to in the city. I thought maybe you wouldn't mind if I came to your apartment."

That cost her—which made him curious as to her motive, wondering if she was purposely setting a meeting on her own terms. Though he'd told his lawyer to give her the address in case she needed to reach him, Heather had never set foot in his apartment or called there.

"All right." He leaned over his desk, propped his elbows on it, and he stared at her picture. In it she was smiling at him, reminding him of everything he'd given up when he'd left her. "What time is good for you?"

She named a time, and he gave her directions. He hesitated breaking the connection, reluctant to end their conversation. But she didn't say anything more, and like a fool, he couldn't think of a way to prolong it. "I'll see you at seven, then."

"Yes," Heather said. "Seven."

Justin put the receiver in its cradle, and a heavy sigh escaped his lips. He drove his fingers through his hair, then held his head in his hands, his eyes fixed on the picture of Heather on his desk. Even after they'd separated, he'd never put it away.

It was of her while they were on their honeymoon. It wasn't one of those posed shots by a professional, but a candid photo, catching her eyes shining with happiness, her wide smile. Her auburn hair fell around her face, and her cheeks were slightly flushed.

She looked happy and blissful.

That had been a lifetime ago, before she'd withdrawn into herself when she'd lost their baby. In the beginning, he'd pushed her, trying to force her to face their loss. When she'd continue to resist his efforts, he'd backed away. He'd dealt with the loss of their child in his own way, throwing himself into his work, driving himself to the edge of sanity just to get through each day. Somehow they'd lost each other in the process of healing their wounds.

But now he hoped they could find the common bond that had brought them together in the beginning of their relationship.

He glanced at his gold watch and realized he had only a few hours before she'd be at his apartment.

Justin decided to step up his plan to woo his wife.

The doorman to the high-rise building didn't hesitate when Heather identified herself and who she was there to see. He opened the door and greeted her cordially, as if they'd met on several occasions before.

"Mrs. Bond. Mr. Bond is expecting you."

She smiled, a nervous little smile that caused her lips to tremble. Obviously Justin had left word with the doorman to expect her. Her legs shaking, she walked across the black-and-white marbled floor to the elevator. Her hand trembled as she pressed the call button. A few moments later, the doors opened and she stepped inside.

Her heart jumped as the car ascended. She told herself it was because of the alarming speed of the elevator, not because it was taking her to Justin. To steady herself, she grasped the silver bar on the wall and held on tight. Before she could regain her equilibrium, the bell sounded and the car stopped on the top floor.

There were several apartment doors in view as she stepped off, but Heather knew to look for the number he'd given her. Still, she glanced at the paper the address was written on to be sure she had it right, then stuffed it inside her purse. She approached the door with the caution a trainer would use when confronting an uncaged lion, then stopped in front of it. Her hand shook as she raised it and gave a soft knock.

Moments later, it opened, and her husband was standing before her. He was dressed rather casually. For Justin, anyway. He had on dark-blue slacks and a polo shirt. His hair was slicked back from his face.

He smiled when he saw her, exposing that adorable dimple, and Heather's heart melted a little, which caused her concern. She resented his ability to generate such a reaction inside her by his mere presence, momentarily robbing her of her perspective.

"Hi," she said, and prayed her legs wouldn't give out on her. Realizing she was clutching her purse, she willed herself to relax. The last thing she wanted was to seem nervous, though at the moment, that was an understatement.

He reached for her hand. She hesitated a beat, then offered it to him.

"Come in," he said, drawing her into the room.

His tense expression relaxed a bit, and she was surprised at the brief look of relief she saw in his eyes. Had he wondered if she would change her mind? Well, it wasn't like she hadn't thought of canceling a hundred times, she admitted silently.

"I was glad to hear from you."

"I said I would call," she reminded him. She felt a tingle of pleasure as his hand closed around hers. It disconcerted her, when more than ever she wanted to keep her bearings about her. The familiar scent of his cologne drifted to her, and unconsciously she stepped closer to him.

Since she'd never been to his apartment, had never even known where it was other than the address, she was more than curious. An odd feeling crawled up her spine as she took in her surroundings. The room was spacious and formal, the furniture expensive and not at all what she'd envisioned. She'd imagined soft leather furniture, black or gray, something appealing to a man, with a large television and every electronic gadget that could possibly be used with it.

Instead, a decorator's touch was evident everywhere, from the modern sofa and chairs, to the valuable framed paintings on the walls and the showy, perfectly placed vases of flowers, statues and lamps.

"I confess that I wondered if you would call."

Her gaze went quickly to his face and an odd feeling made her tremble. The Justin she knew would never have admitted that.

"So this is where you live," she murmured. He seemed totally out of place in the stark surroundings. This could have been anyone's home. There were no signs in the room indicating Justin had made it his home.

"You seem surprised," he said, watching her closely. "Did you think I was living in some luxurious bachelor pad?"

Flushing, she swallowed hard, annoyed he could read her thoughts so easily. "It doesn't even look lived in," she observed, avoiding his comment.

She wasn't surprised that the room was immaculate. Justin had always been obsessively neat. The one time she'd asked him to pick up something he'd left in another room, he'd complied so quickly that he'd stunned her. He'd humbly apologized and sworn it wouldn't happen again. It was such an overreaction that it had caused her concern.

After that day, she'd never had to ask him to pick up behind himself again or even had to remind him to wash out the sink after he shaved. She'd always thought that was a little strange, and she'd broached the subject with him once, but he wouldn't talk about it.

"I've been traveling a lot lately."

His words broke into her thoughts, and he seemed amused by her curiosity. Heather gave him a small smile. "I see."

"Besides the trips to Texas, I've been out of town a lot for the company." Putting his hand behind her back, Justin led her toward a door across the room. "Would you like a drink before dinner?"

"Dinner?" she repeated, then flashed him a confused look.

"I was hoping you hadn't eaten," he told her, ushering her into a large formal dining room. "Have you?"

"No...no, I haven't," she stammered.

He grinned. "Great! I wanted to surprise you."

He'd certainly done that, she thought as she walked inside and examined the room. There was an ornate cherry-wood china cabinet and a matching oval table that could comfortably seat twelve people. Two single candles in crystal heart-shaped bases added atmosphere to what she thought was probably normally an austere room. The table had been set for two, with one place setting at the end and the other to the left.

Touching a switch on the wall, Justin lowered the lights a fraction, adding a touch of ambience. "Here, sit down," he invited, leading her to the side of the table and holding her chair.

Like a robot programmed to follow orders, Heather slid onto a softly padded chair. A single red rose rested across the plate in front of her.

Justin touched her shoulder, then slid his hand with familiar ease to her neck. He leaned over and whispered near her ear, "I'll be right back." Then, before moving away, he murmured, "You smell wonderful."

Heather shivered as he left her. She felt like a bug caught in a spider's web, a tiny little bug facing a really big spider. Apprehension warred with excitement inside her. He'd certainly gone to a lot of trouble for her, and despite her resolve to remain aloof, it touched a tender spot in her heart. This was a side of him she wasn't used to. It made her wonder what else about him had changed.

Fingering the soft petals of the rose, she pondered its intent. Justin had never been what one would call romantic. Though he'd always acknowledged her birthday and their anniversary with gifts, Heather had never felt that he'd put much thought into them. They were never overly personal, and actually, she'd wondered if he'd had his secretary choose them.

Picking up the rose, she breathed in its sweet, floral scent. Justin knew she loved roses, and he'd occasionally brought a dozen home to her. Red roses were her favorite. She trailed the soft, velvet-like petals across her cheek.

Closing her eyes, she remembered the first time he'd given her roses. It had been the night he'd asked her to marry him. From the moment she'd met him, she'd never looked at another man. She'd been thrilled when he proposed.

Now he was proposing something totally different.

The door to the kitchen opened, and heat rushed to her face. She swung her head around in time to see him stop beside her and place two silver covered dishes and a basket of bread on the table. Not wanting him to wonder what suddenly had her hot all over, she quipped, "You cooked?" The truth was, they both knew he'd burn water if it was possible.

That brought a quick smile to his lips. "Smart aleck." His expression was teasing as he lifted the lids and the aroma of garlic and tomato sauce filled the room.

They both laughed, and Heather enjoyed hearing the rich, cheerful sound of his voice. How long had it been since they'd share such a moment? She stared at him, all kinds of raw emotions wreaking havoc inside her.

Life just didn't play fair. When they'd married, she'd thought they'd be happy forever. She supposed that was silly, but it was what she'd longed for, wanted to believe in, despite her father's desertion. It had taken a lot of courage to trust Justin with her heart. What had happened to the love they'd once shared? Where had they failed?

The shared moment died, and as her eyes watered, she looked away.

Justin's lips flattened into a thin line. "What?" he asked as he took his seat. He reached over and touched her hand.

"Nothing."

"Heather—"

She reluctantly turned her gaze to his, her eyes glistening.

"I don't want to hurt you."

"I think I know that," she said, then continued rather solemnly, "in my head. My heart is quite another matter. Sometimes whether we want to or not, we do hurt each other." She stopped speaking to take a breath, to will herself to get control. "I don't know if I can do this again," she admitted truthfully.

"Give us a chance. That's all I'm asking."

She couldn't look at him. "You make it sound so simple, so easy. But it isn't."

Justin let go of her hand and sat back. He breathed heavily. "I don't know what you think, but this past year hasn't been easy for me, either."

"I'm sure it must have been difficult for you too."

She'd seen how the loss of their baby had affected him.

What stunned her now, was that this was the second time he'd disclosed such a private detail to her. This was another example of how he'd changed—something she was going to have to get used to.

He arched a brow. "Are you?" His gaze searched hers. "You're thinking this past year was more difficult for you, though, aren't you?"

Heather *knew* it was. She just couldn't tell him why. Not yet.

Raising Timmy alone, being solely responsible for him, had been demanding, to say the least. But it had been her decision and hers alone. She didn't regret it.

"Not really," she hedged.

He looked as if he didn't believe her. "Why don't we eat?" he suggested, dropping the subject.

She nodded, took a piece of the bread, then offered the basket to him. The bread was warm and smelled wonderful. "This is good," she said, after she'd taken a bite and chewed it.

"You can stop wondering. I have a cook who prepares meals for me when I'm going to be here," Justin explained, opening the bottle of chilled wine.

"Where is she now?" she asked, a small smile playing on her lips.

"She doesn't live here," he explained as he opened the wine bottle. He poured some into a clear crystal goblet in front of her. "She comes in for a few hours at a time, basically whenever I need her." Which wasn't often, he thought to himself. He usually grabbed something to eat before coming back to his apartment to sleep. He didn't like living alone at the apartment. He'd been alone most of his life. He missed the home he'd shared with his wife.

"I'm surprised you can find someone to do that."

"She's paid well. Money has its advantages."

Growing up poor, Justin had thought that money was more important than anything. It wasn't until lately that he'd begun to discover the value of relationships and family. It took meeting the Fortunes to make him cognizant of that. It took missing Heather to drive the message home.

They talked amiably during the rest of the meal, avoiding any mention of the reason they were together. Justin decided not to push her. He hoped that she had decided to come with him to Texas. Why else, he asked himself, would she have come to him? She could have called him if she was going to refuse.

She put her fork down and sipped the remainder of the wine from her glass. He offered her more, but she quickly declined. "I have to drive home."

Justin had other ideas. He wanted to keep her here with him, take her to bed and make slow, passionate love to her. Seducing her hadn't been a part of his original plan, but he was sorely tempted to have her, right then and there.

Her eyes had softened as she relaxed. She licked her lips as she finished the wine in her glass, and he just about came unglued. He wondered if she had any idea of her effect on him. He stirred in his seat, trying to get comfortable.

"I guess we should talk about, you know, things," she suggested. Heather glanced at the ornate clock on the wall. It was late, and she needed to get home. She hated taking advantage of her mother's time. Kathryn had already watched Timmy for hours during the week.

Justin studied her. "Things?"

She stood and walked behind her chair, then braced her hands on the back of it to keep them steady. "I've been thinking a lot about what you suggested."

He folded his arms across his chest. "I'm glad to hear it." She was nervous. He could tell by the way she kept looking away, then back at him. "What have you decided?" he asked, getting right to the point as his breath dammed in his throat.

"That I'll go on several conditions."

Four

"**C**onditions." Justin smelled trouble brewing.

"Yes." Heather nodded, and her hair fell slightly in her face. She brushed it back with her fingers. "First, I'm only agreeing to go to Texas for two weeks."

Two weeks. Justin thought about it. That wasn't as much time as he wanted, but he could step up his plans a little, move a little faster in winning her over. "What else?"

"Wait," Heather cautioned before he could pressure her. "Is that agreeable?"

He got out of his seat and approached her, stopping just a few inches away. "I'll think it over. What else?"

The room fell totally silent as she regarded him. "I don't want you to make any promises that you can't keep."

Justin caught the flicker of pain in her eyes before she was able to conceal it. He guessed he deserved that. "I don't intend to," he whispered fiercely, his gaze cascading over her.

"Sometimes, with the best of intentions, we say things we think the other person wants to hear. I don't want—" she hesitated, biting her lip.

"I want us to be together to see if we can make our marriage work. If it comes down to my hurting you, Heather, I'll back off. You have my word."

"So, if after two weeks, things don't work out between us, you'll give me a divorce?" This had to be clear between them. She'd spent a year repairing the damage to her heart. She wasn't going to do it again. Lord help her, she *couldn't* do it again.

"Yes."

"All right."

"Is that all?" he asked. He fingered a strand of her hair, then frowned when she backed away.

She cleared her throat. "Well, no, not exactly."

"There's more?" Justin asked, surprised.

Heather backed another step away from him. "I won't make love with you."

Momentarily confused, he scratched his ear. "You mean *no* sex?"

"If you must put it bluntly, yes."

"No sex." He said it again, as if to convince himself that he'd heard her right. Or perhaps by hearing it, he could agree to it, convince himself it was possible. Fat chance! He wanted her now, had even thought of seducing her the moment she'd walked through the door.

"We're trying to put our marriage back together,"

she reminded him, rationalizing, "I don't think we should confuse our feelings with sex."

Justin felt as if he'd been dealt a blow to his lower body with a sledgehammer. Tension clamped his stomach muscles. "And we can't put our marriage back together *with* sex?"

"Don't be deliberately obtuse," she retorted, glaring at him with irritation. "You know *exactly* what I mean. We have a lot to talk about, a lot to work out. It's not going to be easy being with each other again, and I don't want to confuse what we're going through—trying to accomplish—by making love."

Justin couldn't disagree more with her logic. Making love could only bring them closer to recommitting. For himself, hell, he just wanted her writhing naked beneath him. His loins responded immediately from the mental vision of the two of them making love, and he had to forcibly rein in his desire to drag her into his arms and show her how good they were together.

Damn! He gnawed at the inside of his lip. Now what?

"You're sure this is what you want?" he asked, hoping, *praying,* she'd reconsider. He couldn't imagine spending a day, much less two weeks, without touching her soft skin, kissing her lush lips. He'd counted on using their natural attraction to each other to win her back, and he was more than anxious to reestablish their sex life.

"Yes."

He gave her a rough smile. "You drive a hard bargain." He hadn't been prepared for this, and he didn't like being caught off guard. So far she'd surprised him. She'd controlled their meeting place, as well as the conditions of their reconciliation.

"Then you agree?"

"I guess I have to. You seem to have me at a disadvantage." Not for long, he thought, already reassessing his strategy. She hadn't said anything about touching. Or kissing.

Or sleeping arrangements.

He wasn't going to remind her, either. Not until he got a commitment from her to go to Texas. He'd agree to anything to get her to spend some time alone together, away from the bad memories lingering between them.

"All right, I'll go with you."

"Ah, Heather," Justin murmured on an achingly wistful sigh. "You won't be sorry." He slipped his hand around her neck, and his fingers massaged her skin.

"Justin." She raised her arm and brushed his hand away. Picking up her purse, she said, "It's getting late. I should be getting home. Um, thank you for dinner."

He gave her a tight smile. "You're welcome." He followed her out the dining room door and into the living room. "We haven't discussed when we can leave. I'd like to call Miranda so she'll know when to expect us."

"I have a week of school left," Heather explained, thinking of everything she had to do for her first-grade students. Though she'd had Timmy during the second half of the school year and could have stayed out the remainder, she'd chosen to return to finish the year. She'd wanted to see her students move on to the next grade. Thankfully, she had a teacher assistant to help her as she made the adjustment back to full-time work. "But I can be ready in about eight days, if you like."

"All right." Before she had a chance to turn from him, Justin caught her arm, then pulled her toward him.

"I've missed you, Heather," he professed, drawing her into his embrace.

Startled by his admission, she looked up at him, wanting to believe him. But he'd walked away from her once. Mistrust cautioned her that he was capable of doing so again. "Have you?" She put her hands on his chest, then lightly pushed out of his arms. "You sure could have fooled me."

The telephone was ringing as Heather came in the door from school. She deposited Timmy in his corner on the kitchen floor, handed him a toy to distract him, then hurriedly grabbed the extension on the wall.

"Hello," she answered, breathless.

"Heather, it's Justin."

She felt a rush of excitement at the sound of his deep voice. He'd only been back in her life for three days, and already he was causing chaos with her emotions. Heather felt as if she were on a rollercoaster ride, one that kept going around and around and wouldn't let her off.

"Hi," she said, and wondered why he was calling. They'd agreed on leaving the day after school was out.

After she'd left him, she'd been exhausted—still was, for that matter. The drive back to her mom's to pick up Timmy, then going home and putting him, and herself, to bed had taken its toll after a full day at work.

"I called to offer my services."

Mystified, she asked, "For what?"

"I thought you might need some help packing. I know you're busy, like you said, finishing up the school year. Is there something I can do to help you?"

The last thing Heather wanted was Justin underfoot. She searched for a reasonable excuse. Besides needing a day to recoup her resolve not to let their relationship move too fast, she had to keep Timmy a secret from Justin for just a while longer. She felt she had to give the two of them this time together to see if they could salvage their relationship, without the bond of a child to complicate their feelings. Having him come over to help pack her things or get the house ready would make that impossible.

"I don't think so, but I appreciate the offer. I think I have everything under control."

"Then I'd like to take you to dinner. I thought maybe you'd like to know a little more about my family, and we could discuss our travel plans."

"Oh, Justin, I don't know." She started to say she had too much to do, but caught herself. Hadn't she just assured him everything was fine?

"We're going to be with each other pretty much every minute for the next two weeks. Don't you think we need to spend a little time getting reacquainted?" he said reasonably.

His suggestion made more sense than she cared to admit. Her heart began beating hard and fast at the thought of seeing him, being with him again. No matter how often she reminded herself to take it slow, her heart just wouldn't listen.

* * *

At seven that evening, Justin turned in to Heather's driveway and cut the engine of his Mercedes sedan. His entire body felt tense. He looked through the windshield of the car at the house they had shared together, and a flood of memories assailed him. Most of them good, some of them sharp and infinitely painful.

The last few months of living with her had been sheer hell for him. He'd been unable to reach her through her pain. Living with her indifference was a constant reminder of that failure to reach her.

It was as if *he* hadn't mattered to her anymore, and that had hurt him more than anything. He had lived through rejection many times: each time he'd been taken from a foster home, he'd learned to harden his heart and deal with it.

But enduring rejection from Heather had devastated him. At a time when he'd needed her the most, she'd turned away from him. Justin wanted back the life they'd once had. He wanted to be with his wife, to hold her, to spend the rest of his life taking care of her.

And dammit, he wanted to make love to her!

Justin knew he was in trouble. Already he wanted her to the point of distraction. He had to sit in the car another few minutes to let his body calm down. When he thought he could face her without making a fool of himself, he got out and approached the house. Though he had the right to just walk inside, he rang the doorbell and waited for her to answer.

After a moment, she opened the door and stepped back to allow him to enter. Her expression was apprehensive, yet he caught the flare of awareness that passed through her eyes as their gazes met.

"Hi."

Damn! His gaze drifted over her, taking in her curvaceous figure and her sexy legs. He smiled appreciatively, then leaned forward and kissed her cheek. She tilted her head for him, then quickly stepped back.

"You smell delicious." Justin's heart responded with a quick beat to the unique scent of her. She always wore a delicate fragrance that reminded him of roses. He breathed deeply, taking in her fragrance again before moving away.

She blushed, seeming pleased that he'd noticed and had spoken his thoughts. Her smile widened to her eyes.

"Come in."

He walked into the living room. "I hope I'm not early. I can wait if you have something to finish." He glanced around the room and saw no evidence that she was preparing to leave. It was spotless, as if she'd spent the afternoon cleaning rather than packing.

Heather followed him. Her gaze automatically scanned the room, then she looked at him. "No, I've done all I can do for the night. I'm really tired, so I needed a break. Thanks for offering to take me to dinner."

A small object on the floor near the sofa caught her eye, and she realized it was a rattle. Frantic, her gaze shot to his face to see if he'd noticed it. Breathing a sigh of relief when she realized he hadn't, she smiled brightly, then walked across the room and stopped beside the toy.

"Um, I didn't ask before," she began, placing her

foot in front of the toy and blocking it from his view, "how are you handling business while you're in San Antonio?" She moved her foot a fraction and felt the rattle roll slightly. She also thought she'd heard it. Alarmed, she glanced up quickly.

"I have a laptop, and the hotel I stay in has fax and Internet services. It won't be a problem. I'll be accessible, but I don't expect to be working much of the time."

He was taking their trip together seriously. A pleasurable feeling rushed over her. Needing to distract him to scoot the rattle under the sofa, she said, "I wasn't sure how to dress. You didn't say where we were going." She moved her foot a fraction at a time, edging Timmy's rattle under the sofa.

Whew! That was close, she thought. She was going to have to be more careful.

Justin's gaze slipped over her body and down her legs. Her light-blue dress stopped just above her knees, and she wore white heels that accentuated her slender legs. He remembered the times she'd wrapped those legs around him while in the throes of passion.

Hell, they'd made love right on the living room floor more than once. He hardened, aware even more of how much he missed being intimate with her, sliding into her warm, wet body. She turned slightly, and her dress swished around her thighs. "You look great."

"Thanks." Heather had taken the time to change into something attractive for dinner, and because she'd be seeing him. As a rule, she didn't dress up for school. She'd learned early on in her career that six-year-old children could destroy a dress with one touch of a hand colored in fingerpaint. "Well, I'm ready to leave if you are."

Justin wanted to tell her what he was really ready to do. Instead, he clamped down on his basic urges, nodded, then followed her when she walked to the door and stepped outside. After seating her in his car, he joined her, sliding in behind the wheel. "I thought we'd go to Angelo's."

Startled, Heather looked at him. "Angelo's?" She'd said it before she was able to subdue her astonished tone. Angelo's was the restaurant where Justin had proposed to her.

A ripple of pleasure stole her breath. She was both surprised and pleased he'd chosen to take her there. Or was she reading too much into this? Feeling silly about being so nostalgic, she looked away from him and out the window of the car.

"I hope that's all right." He sent a questioning look her way before turning his attention back to the road. He'd hoped she'd be pleased that he'd chosen a place where they had shared a special moment in their lives. It was part of his plan to remind her of a time when things were easy between them.

Glancing back at him, she smiled and relaxed a little. "Of course it is. I'm looking forward to it."

When they arrived at the restaurant, Heather was stunned when they were seated at the exact same table they'd had on the night he'd asked her to marry him. It was either a bizarre coincidence, or a well thought-out plan.

She looked across the table at him and swallowed the lump in her throat. He wore a black suit, and exuded confidence and determination. Several women had turned to look at them as they'd moved through the room. Heather had felt their stares, and she'd been aware of her own pleasure at being the object of their envy.

Her chest ached with a tension born of a year of keeping a staggering secret. She couldn't believe that she was sitting across from her husband and having dinner. Her husband, who had walked out on her without looking back.

She'd wondered at the time if another woman had been involved, but had never seen any evidence that he hadn't been faithful. That left the year they'd lived apart for her to ponder. Who had he been with? Had another woman comforted him, made love to him? Did Heather even want to know? Could she take him back not knowing?

The waiter stopped by, took their drink orders, then disappeared just as quickly. She fingered her linen napkin as she glanced around the room.

"So the packing is going well?" Justin asked, watching her fiddle with her napkin. She gave no indication that there was anything special about the restaurant. Disappointment shattered the pleasure he'd felt upon deciding to bring her here. He'd hoped she'd say something, *anything,* to let him know she remembered the night he'd proposed.

"Um, yes." Her smile was anxious, her eyes perplexed.

Justin nodded, trying to get past the deflation of his ego. "And school is over in four days?"

"Three, actually. After classes end, I have a day to pack up my classroom."

The waiter returned with their drinks and took their orders. Heather watched him walk away, then looked back at her husband.

"Why don't I stop by to help you?"

"What?" She stared blankly at him. He'd always been too busy at work to help her with anything remotely related to her job. She'd even had to drag him to school functions that she'd been required to attend. "I'm sure you have some last-minute things at work to take care of," she blurted, her tone discouraging.

She couldn't take a chance on anyone at school talking to Justin. Heather was a very private person, and though some of her school colleagues knew about her separation, she'd never shared the information that her husband didn't know about his son. No, she didn't need Justin stopping by the school.

"Not really."

"Well, I appreciate the offer, but I don't have too much left to do. And my assistant has been tremendously helpful. She's been putting in some extra hours and has done most of the work." She hoped her excuse sounded reasonable.

"Well, let me know if you change your mind."

"Oh, of course, thank you."

An uncomfortable silence fell between them. After a few moments, they began talking about their travel plans while they waited for the food to arrive. Once it was served, Heather was relieved to have something to do with her hands. She wrapped some fettuccine around her fork and ate it, moaning pleasurably as the flavor of butter and Parmesan cheese reached her palate.

"I'd forgotten how good Angelo's food is," she offered, trying to ease the tension that had somehow overshadowed their evening.

"You haven't been here in a while?"

Sadness darkened her eyes. "Not since we were

last here together.'' She couldn't tell him that she hadn't been able to come here without him.

Justin reached across the table to touch her hand. He ran one finger over the top of it with slow stroking motions. "I haven't, either," he confessed.

Though he'd taken a few women to dinner since his separation, he hadn't slept with any of them. He'd been damn tempted to assuage his sexual urges a few times, but Heather had always insinuated herself into his thoughts, and he'd ended up going home alone.

Now he was glad he had, was relieved a sexual affair wasn't something that could come between them.

Heather drew her hand back and sipped some wine. "Tell me a little more about the Fortunes."

Justin described them as best he could, then told her more about Emma and her baby, Rose, and her recent marriage to Flynn Sinclair.

"She sounds very nice." Heather lifted another forkful of noodles from her plate. "Will I get to meet her?"

"Probably, and her baby," he added, his tone cautious. "Will that be difficult for you?"

To learn that he was concerned for her emotional well-being touched Heather deeply, but it also added to the burden of guilt in her heart. "No, I'll be fine," she managed to get out past the lump in her throat. Beads of perspiration dotted her upper lip.

Justin thought he'd noticed something different about her manner. He shouldn't have brought up the subject of Rose. It had probably stirred agonizing memories for his wife, memories she hadn't laid to rest.

The subject of Emma's baby seem to cloud the

remainder of their evening. Though they talked, Heather seemed reserved and quiet. Justin accepted that she might still have wounds to heal. He knew he did. He still thought about the baby they'd lost, still wished...

When they arrived back at her house after dinner, he walked her to the door. They'd said little to each other on the ride home, and he hadn't tried to initiate casual conversation. Heather had seemed deep in thought, which was natural. They were both going through a difficult transition.

At the door, she turned, lifting her face to look up at him. "Thank you. Dinner was lovely."

Justin stared at her. She was so beautiful, but wariness lingered in her eyes. He swallowed hard, clamping down on the desire to pull her to him. "I guess that means you're not going to invite me in."

She slowly shook her head. "I have a big day tomorrow. I hope you understand."

All Justin could understand at the moment was how much he wanted her. He stepped toward her and felt electricity spark between them. She felt it, too. He could see it in her eyes as they darkened under the dim porch light. She edged away as he came closer, stopping only when her back hit the door.

"Heather." Her name was a whisper as he bent toward her. Her head came up, her gaze resting on his face, reflecting a mixture of need and denial. He didn't touch her, but it took every ounce of willpower not to. "I want to kiss you."

She stared at him without speaking. He waited a beat, then lowered his mouth, touching hers briefly. Then he raised his head a fraction.

"Justin."

Instead of a protest, he heard a request. Her warm breath fanned his lips, and a need, deep and burning, engulfed him. Then he was kissing her. Softly, tenderly, achingly. She opened her mouth to him, and he slid his tongue past the barrier of her teeth to tease and taste and devour. She leaned into him, softly pressing her hands against his chest.

Not wanting to push too hard too fast, Justin lifted his lips and looked at her.

"You don't play fair," she whispered, her breathing labored.

"You set the rules," he remind her. He briefly kissed her lips again, then stepped back, putting some distance between them. He knew it was what she wanted, despite her reaction to his kiss. "Not kissing you wasn't one of them."

Five

Heather's heart was beating hard against her ribs as she watched Justin walk away. She turned and went inside, as he drove off in his car. Entering the dark and quiet house, she walked immediately to Timmy's room and peeked in to check on him. He was sleeping on his back in the crib. She crept over to him and stared down at her beautiful little boy, who looked so much like his father. God, she was so fortunate to have him. So very blessed.

He'd brought her joy and happiness at a time when she'd thought she'd never be able to feel either emotion again. She wanted Timmy to do the same for Justin, wanted him to heal Justin's heart from the pain of losing their first child. She vowed to herself and to her son to tell his father about him soon.

Sighing wistfully, she left the room to find her

mother. She met Kathryn in the hall outside Timmy's room.

"I thought I heard you."

"I was checking on Timmy. Did he give you any problems?"

"Of course not. He went right to sleep when I put him down." She looked at her daughter with concern. "Is everything all right?"

"I guess." Heather shrugged. "I don't know. I feel so mixed up inside," she confessed, sounding miserable.

"That's only natural. You've had quite a lot to think about over the past couple of days."

"I know you're right, but—" She stopped speaking and massaged her temples.

"Come on." Kathryn took her daughter's hand and tugged her toward the kitchen. "Let's get you something for your head, then I'll make you some herbal tea."

Heather let her mother lead her, then, exhaustion consuming her, took a seat at the table.

"How was your dinner?" Kathryn gave Heather a glass of water and some pills for her headache.

"It was nice. I enjoyed myself most of the time. Justin seems…so different in some ways."

"People change," Kathryn offered, "sometimes for the better." She put a cup of water in the microwave and punched in a time. When the microwave finished heating the water, Heather watched her mother get a tea bag from the cupboard and put it in the steaming cup. Her mom was right. Justin had a hard-edged manner, was sometimes too sure of himself and often too possessive. But he was also confident and reliable. Heather supposed it was one of the reasons his leaving had hurt her so much. She'd relied on him to see her through the pain of her miscarriage. He'd disappointed her.

"I want to believe that. I still have feelings for him. I just don't know if what I feel and what he feels is enough."

Kathryn nodded as if she understood. "One thing you need to remember is that you and Justin have something between you that makes it worth a try." She nodded toward the back of the house where her grandson was sleeping. "Your son."

"It's not always the right decision to stay together because of children. Sometimes that can create even more chaos."

"Oh, I'll agree with you. I wouldn't have stayed with your father because of you," she admitted honestly. "But if he had loved me, I might have tried to save my marriage."

"Do you think you could have trusted him again?"

"I don't know. Trust never comes easily after someone has hurt you. Listen," Kathryn said, putting the tea in front of Heather. "There's a commitment involved with marriage that people make to each other. You have to really and truly believe in it if your marriage is going to work." She got to her feet. "I'd better get going. Do you need any help tomorrow?"

Heather walked with her mother to the front door. "No thanks, Mom. You've done enough. Are you really sure you want to keep Timmy while I go to San Antonio?"

Kathryn rolled her eyes. "Yes, for the umpteenth time. I have leave at work that I'll lose if I don't take it, so it's no problem. Honey, he'll be fine. I promise.

And you can call anytime you want to check on him.''

Heather's smile wavered. ''I know he'll be in good hands. I'm just nervous about leaving him.''

And about being with his father.

''I know you said you didn't need any help, but I thought I'd stop by and take you to lunch.''

Justin! Heather froze in the process of filling a box with the items from her school desk, then spun around. He was standing in the doorway to her classroom, casually leaning against the doorjamb in not-so-casual attire. Again he was dressed in a suit, this one charcoal-gray with a white silk shirt and gray silk tie. He looked as attractive as ever, and a tremor of excitement flowed through her at the sight of him. Her hands shaking, Heather put the item in her hand in the box—before she dropped and broke it.

Thank goodness she'd already cleared her desk of pictures of Timmy! Forcing a smile to her lips, she let her gaze find his. ''You really didn't need to stop by,'' she assured him, and tried not to sound ungrateful. She was just so afraid one of her colleagues would stop in, see him and say something *she'd* regret.

Justin strolled into the room, his gaze taking in the bare walls and the tables with small plastic chairs stacked on top of them. ''I see you weren't kidding. You've about done everything, huh?''

She approached him reluctantly, as if facing a firing squad. ''Yes. I'm just finishing up.'' Each teacher was responsible for breaking down her classroom so it could be used for summer school. Anything of value, they took with them on the last day. ''I'm taking this box home," she continued, pointing to the cardboard box on top of her desk. She walked over and quickly tossed the last few items in, then closed the lid.

"Are you about ready to leave? I'll take it to your car."

Heather glanced around the room, thankful she'd come in early. If she hadn't, there's was no telling what Justin would have seen. She snatched up her purse, not realizing it was open until the contents spilled out in disarray on the desk.

"Oh!" Furious at herself, she grasped at the items, trying to prevent them from falling onto the floor.

"Let me help you," Justin grinned. He stopped a pen from rolling off the desk, then caught a compact before it, too, fell.

Timmy's pacifier! She spotted the little blue soother that she kept in her purse for emergencies, just as Justin's hand started to reach for it. When he realized what it was, his gaze shot to hers, his eyebrows embedded in a deep frown.

Thinking quickly, she blurted out, "Um, that's my friend's. I baby-sat for her one evening, and she left it at my house." She nibbled on her bottom lip. "I've been meaning to give it back to her, but I keep forgetting."

The frown left his face slowly. Shrugging, he picked up the pacifier and handed it to her.

That was too close. Heather stuffed it in her purse with everything else, then snapped it shut. Mortified, she chanced a quick glance at Justin, but he didn't seem at all suspicious. Clearing her throat, she motioned toward the door. "I guess I'm ready to leave."

Justin nodded, then picked up the box and followed her to her car. He deposited the box in her trunk, then

walked to the driver's door. Using the key, she unlocked the door, but Justin's hand was on it before
she had a chance to open it. She turned, then lifted
her face to look at him.

"It was nice of you to stop by."

He held on to the door, preventing her from opening it enough to get inside. "Is there anything I can
help you with at the house?"

Heather pretended to think about it, knowing there
was no way she could let him come to the house. Her
mother was going to bring Timmy home, then stay to
help her finish packing. Planning to live at Heather's
while she was gone, Kathryn had already brought
most of her things over. "No. Really, I've got it about
done. Besides, Mom is coming by tonight."

Justin leaned forward a little, resting his weight
against the open door. The mention of her mother's
name brightened his usual serious expression. "How
is Kathryn?"

Heather smiled. "She's doing fine."

"What did you tell her?"

"About us? The truth." She didn't want any other
secrets between them. "This past year hasn't been
easy emotionally. She's been there for me more times
than I can count."

Translated, that meant that she'd had a difficult
time getting through the breakup of their marriage.
Justin hoped to wipe the past year from her memory.
Was it too much to ask? Would he be able to convince her they still had a chance to repair the damage
they had done to each other?

"I'm glad she was there for you." Unlike Heather,
he'd had no one to turn to. Not that he would have
shared what he felt with anyone. He'd learned a long

time ago to depend on himself and no one else, and he saw no reason to change that philosophy just because he'd met his birth mother and siblings.

Some things couldn't be undone with time. Justin hoped his marriage didn't fall into that category.

He raised a brow. "I guess you told her about going to Texas."

Nodding, she said, "She's going to keep an eye on the house for me while I'm gone. I also mentioned to her that you'd met your biological mother." She slid her hand along his arm, then quickly withdrew it. "She was very happy for you, too."

Justin could imagine that Kathryn would be. Other than Heather, she was the only other person who had seemed genuinely to care about him. How did she feel about him now? he wondered. He'd walked back into her daughter's life without warning. More than likely, Kathryn was questioning his motives.

He couldn't blame her. He'd questioned his own and hadn't come up with any definitive answers.

"Tell her hello for me. I'd like to see her when we get back."

"I'm sure she'd like to see you, too." Heather glanced around the deserted parking lot. Like her, most of the teachers had arrived early so they could be gone by noon. She knew the rest of the day would fly by, and she still had a lot to do to get ready for the trip. Most of all, she wanted to spend time with Timmy tonight. She still couldn't believe she was leaving her baby for two weeks. Swallowing hard, she forced back the tears that threatened to appear in her eyes.

"I guess I'll see you in the morning." He was reluctant to leave her, couldn't quell the fear in the back of his mind that it was possible she'd change her mind. His heart wrenched at the thought.

"Sure." She moved to push the door open. Justin held it in place, which again drew her eyes to his.

He leaned forward and gently kissed her mouth. "Thank you for agreeing to go and for taking another chance on us," he whispered.

Heather looked at him, and at that moment she truly believed they *did* have a fighting chance. Touching his hand, she let her gaze drift over his face, and she remembered how easily she'd fallen for him seven years ago. "I'm glad you came to see me." That was all she could say, truthfully. It was all that she was willing to share. She wanted to believe in him this time, wanted to believe he wouldn't hurt her again, yet mistrust lingered in her heart. "I'll see you in the morning."

As she drove home, Heather painfully revisited the option of telling Justin about his son. She knew that if she did, he'd *insist* on making their marriage work, rather than giving them time to see if it would. She wanted this opportunity with him to discover his true feelings for her. Would keeping Timmy's birth from her husband be the right means to an end?

When he found out the truth, would he forgive her?

Heather wasn't sure, but she knew she had to do this her way. Her entire future was on the line, as was Justin's.

And her baby's.

"I don't think I can go through with this." Cradling Timmy in her arms, Heather paced the tiled floor in front of the cooking island in her spacious kitchen. She pressed a kiss to his chubby cheek, then brushed her chin back and forth across his soft brown hair. "Why did I ever believe I could leave Timmy?"

Panic began to consume her, and her heart pumped spastically. "I just can't do this!" Her expression was frantic as she faced her mother.

Kathryn glanced pointedly at her watch. "This is a fine time to think about changing your mind. Justin should be here in just a few minutes."

A stricken expression ignited in Heather's eyes. "I can't. I just...what if something happens and I'm all the way across the country? He could get hurt, or what if he catches something and gets sick?"

Kathryn rolled her eyes. "Calm down, honey. Timmy will be fine. He'll be with me, and you know I wouldn't let anything happen to him."

"I know you won't, Mom, but something beyond your control could happen. What if you're in an accident in the car and he's hurt?" She was beginning to sound neurotic, but she couldn't stop herself.

Kathryn tried to reason with her. "That could happen if you were the one driving." She blocked her daughter's path, preventing her from moving. "Look, honey, life is full of unknowns. You've got to pull yourself together."

"Oh, Mom—"

"Well," Kathryn stated pragmatically, "you can always tell him about Timmy."

Heather paled. "No!"

"Then take a deep breath and calm down before Justin gets here. You've gone out on a long limb to make this work. Are you saying you're willing to throw that all away? If you don't pull yourself together, he's going to wonder what's wrong with you."

That was the last thing Heather needed right now. She followed her mother's advice and breathed in deeply, letting out the air in her lungs slowly.

"Now, I'll take really good care of Timmy. He'll be just fine. You can call every day to check on him."

"I know. It's just that I haven't been away from him before." She lovingly stroked her baby's head.

"Well, this is for a good reason, right?"

Heather nodded.

"Then it'll be worth it when everything works out."

"You mean *if*."

"I mean *when*. I have every belief that you and Justin *will* work things out." Her gaze searched her daughter's face. "You still care for him, don't you?"

"Yes, I still feel something for him. If I didn't, I wouldn't be doing this," Heather admitted. "I just don't know if—"

"This isn't the time for doubting yourself, Heather. Just take it slow and easy these next couple of weeks. If Justin didn't care for you, he wouldn't have come back. When he found out about his family, he wanted to share it with *you*. And he wants them to know you. That means he still has deep feelings for you."

"I hope you're right." Her tone sounded unsure even to her.

The doorbell chimed, and she jumped as if she'd received an electric shock. "That's Justin!" She hugged Timmy close, then kissed his face all over. "Be a good boy, honey. Mommy will be back soon."

Kathryn took the baby, and Heather gathered her purse and carry-on bag. "Mom, thank you so much," she whispered, hugging her fiercely. "I love you."

"I love you, too. Now, go. Don't keep him waiting.

He may want to come inside. I'll stay here and keep Timmy out of sight.''

''Thanks, Mom. I know you're uncomfortable about this, but I appreciate your help.'' She hated having to involve her mother in her deceit.

''You're welcome. Try and have a great time.'' She shooed her daughter out of the kitchen and toward the foyer.

Heather reached the front door as the bell chimed again. Stopping, she closed her eyes, sucking in a deep breath. Then she lifted her eyes as she opened the door.

Her gaze swept over her husband, causing her heart to lurch in a way that was becoming all-too-familiar when he was around. He'd shed his usual business attire for a conservative patterned sport coat, a polo shirt and matching trousers. His idea of casual.

She stepped onto the porch, and quickly pulled the door shut behind her. As the June heat hit her, she was glad she'd chosen to wear a lemon-yellow sundress and white sandals. Justin looked so fresh and collected, and not at all disturbed by the hot weather. He had so much control, she figured he just decided he wouldn't let the heat bother him—and so it didn't.

''Hi.''

Justin kissed her cheek, and his lips lingered a mo ment longer than necessary. Heather's nerve endings burned.

''You're ready?'' he asked.

She didn't miss the tone of astonishment in his voice. ''I haven't forgotten that you're punctual,'' she replied, and she gave him a teasing smile. During their marriage, they'd had a few heated discussions over the merits of being on time, mainly because she hadn't been especially organized and had often made them late.

"And I haven't forgotten how you always made me stand around and wait."

He winked at her, and she lost another little piece of her heart. His relaxed manner was such a direct contrast to his normally reserved demeanor that she felt goose bumps prickle her skin.

"You mean 'pace.'"

"Whatever."

He grinned briefly, flashing that adorable dimple at her, and butterflies fluttered in her stomach. Was it going to be like this now? she wondered. Would it be like when they first met? Flirting with each other, taking time to get to know one another again?

He picked up her cases, which she'd put on the porch earlier, and started for the car. She fell into step beside him. When he pressed a button on his key chain, the trunk popped open, and he placed her luggage in with his. She walked to the side of the car as he shut the trunk, but before she could reach for the handle, Justin was beside her and opening the door.

She felt the brief touch of his hand on her shoulder as she got in the car, and it sent a wave of warmth through her that had nothing to do with the weather and everything to do with him.

He went around the car and seated himself, then started the engine. Heather glanced at him, then made work of adjusting her seat belt—anything she could do to settle her nerves.

Only days ago she had been contemplating how she was going to spend her summer. Now she didn't have an inkling as to what was going to happen in the next few hours. The only thing she was sure about was that she was going to miss her baby.

She looked at the house, as the car backed out of the driveway. The curtain on one of the windows in the living room moved and caught her eye. Her mother was standing there, peeking out. The older woman moved slightly, just barely showing Timmy in her arms, and Heather had to swallow hard to prevent the sob that formed deep inside.

Oh, God! Please take care of him! She fought back the sudden tears that stung her eyes and tried to cover her anxiety by staring quietly out the window. Justin made conversation on the drive to the airport, but by the time they arrived and parked, she couldn't even remember what he'd said.

Until they were seated in first-class on the plane, she thought she'd handled her emotions pretty well. But when the airplane's wheels left the ground and the finality of her separation from her baby became real, tears sprang to her eyes. She clutched the armrests with her hands and turned her head away, trying very hard to act normal even as she was coming apart inside.

Justin had been staring blankly out the window of the airplane when he heard Heather sniff. He turned to look at her, his expression curious.

She was crying!

"Are you all right?" he asked, his expression full of concern.

"I'm fine." Her tone was raspy, as if she had a sore throat.

Reaching into a pocket of his sport coat, he retrieved a white handkerchief. "Here." He was at a loss for words. What was going on? Had he done or said something to upset her?

She took the handkerchief without looking at him, and he frowned. Going back over their conversation during the ride to the airport, he could think of nothing he'd said that would cause her to be so upset.

He reached over and linked their fingers together, holding her hand tightly. "Do you want to talk?" he asked quietly, trying to be supportive.

She shook her head. "Not really." The tears came faster.

Justin absently rubbed his thumb across the top of her hand. She didn't want to talk to him, didn't want to tell him what had upset her. He pondered the wisdom of forcing the issue. While he wanted Heather to need him, opening up, talking, was still difficult for them both. He knew it would take time for them to share what they were feeling about this reunion.

He felt dejected, and scolded himself for it. Maybe he'd been too cocky believing he could whisk his wife away so they could be alone to try to repair the damage they'd done to their lives.

Maybe it *wasn't* that simple. What if he was wrong? What if he caused them both more pain and heartache in the end? Could he live with knowing he'd hurt her once again?

Was he taking too much for granted by banking on their physical attraction to each other? He knew she still felt something for him, but was it enough? He didn't want to think about the possibility that Heather didn't care for him somewhere deep in her heart.

So he wouldn't have to face an issue he wasn't prepared to deal with, he turned his thoughts in another direction. Maybe she was anxious about meeting his mother and the rest of the Fortunes. He'd told Heather a little about them, and figured their wealth could be intimidating.

Justin had been honest with Miranda when she'd first questioned him about his wife. It had been right after Emma's wedding when she'd mentioned noticing his wedding band. Up to that moment, he hadn't shared many details of his life with any of the Fortunes. Justin had simply told Miranda that he was married. When he didn't offer further details, she didn't push, but mentioned she'd like to meet his wife.

Since he'd met his mother, Justin had visited her on several occasions. Each time, he'd found her a little easier to be with, but he still hadn't gotten past his resentment of the way she'd abandoned her children.

She'd explained in detail how she'd purposely left Justin and Emma on the steps to a sheriff's office, thinking that they'd be adopted. She'd insisted that she had no idea they would end up in foster care for their entire childhood. Still, it was hard for Justin to erase the feeling of having been deserted.

When Miranda first asked to meet Heather, Justin hadn't even considered asking her to come to Texas. He didn't know if she would come, and at the time, his family didn't know about her miscarriage and the difficulty the tragedy had brought upon them both.

But during subsequent trips to visit his mother and the rest of his family, Justin had begun to observe them closely. He'd seen how happy Emma was when she married Flynn. Feeling envious, he began to examine his feelings for Heather, and he discovered he still cared very deeply for her.

That's when he'd decided on a plan to win her back.

She sniffed again, catching his attention and bringing him back to the present. He wanted to tell her not to worry, to promise her that everything would be all right. But he couldn't. He'd already told her he wouldn't make promises he couldn't keep. Steeling his heart, he reminded himself that it was possible they wouldn't make it. He didn't like the sick feeling in his stomach when his mind registered that thought.

Six

"Where are we staying?" Heather asked, once they were in a cab and headed away from San Antonio International Airport.

"I have a suite at one of the hotels along the River Walk." He told the driver the name of the hotel.

"River Walk is in the heart of downtown San Antonio, not too far from Kingston Estates, where Miranda lives." He knew how much Heather loved plants, and he tried to explain what the River Walk looked like. "You'll see. We'll tour it a little once we're settled in."

"The Alamo's nearby, isn't it?" she asked, recalling that the area had deep ties to America's history.

"Within walking distance." He reached over and clasped her hand. "Would you like to see it?"

"Oh, yes!"

Her face lit up, and Justin's chest tightened. He

wanted to lean over and kiss her luscious mouth right then and there, but stopped himself short. Take it slow. He had to give her time to adjust to the changes they were going through.

Him? Well, hell, he didn't need to adjust to anything where she was concerned. He'd always thought she was beautiful, so much so that he had trouble breathing around her. While they were married, he'd tried to make her happy, but it had been hard to let down the walls around his heart—even with her. Was that where he'd gone wrong?

Had he changed enough to save his marriage?

"Then we will," he said. "That's a promise I can keep." He winked at her, playing with her, and she gave him a full smile that reached her eyes and made the corners crinkle. "I haven't forgotten anything we discussed, sweetheart."

Sweetheart. He hadn't called her that in...so long Heather couldn't even remember the last time. She couldn't even recall the last endearment he had used for her. She remembered only the silence, the emptiness that had consumed her, the feeling of being so terribly alone.

He gently squeezed her hand, as the cab pulled to a stop in front of the hotel entrance. Then he got out, went around and opened her door.

Heather glanced around her. It was early afternoon. They'd had an unexpected short layover in Chicago. She felt tired and exhausted. Sighing heavily, she wished for a few minutes to rest.

She waited as Justin made arrangements to have their luggage brought to his suite, then walked inside the hotel with him.

The hotel boasted a large yet welcoming lobby, a

lavish area with shiny tiled floors. Her sandals made a clicking sound as she crossed to the elevators. After a few moments, the doors opened and they stepped inside. She wasn't surprised when Justin punched the button for the top floor.

Her heart started beating faster, as if to keep pace with the elevator as it raced upward. When the doors opened, there were two hallways.

Curious, she asked, "How many suites are on this floor?"

"I'm not sure. But they're pretty big. And very private."

Which explained why he was staying at this hotel, she thought. He'd never liked crowds, preferred to keep to himself. While they were married, they hadn't really made many friends, and they rarely went out with anyone, unless it had to do with business.

She trailed slightly behind him as they approached his suite. He slipped a magnetic card into the lock, then turned the knob at the sound of a *click*. Standing aside, Justin ushered her in, then followed. He tossed the hotel room card on a nearby table.

Heather glanced around the sitting room. It was much like a luxurious apartment, with an overstuffed sofa and a matching chair in front of a television, a couple of tables and lamps and a decent-size desk. On the left was a beautiful glass table with matching chairs. There was also a kitchen area, complete with a microwave and coffeepot. Over in the corner she spotted a wet bar.

"Are you tired? Hungry?"

She turned her head in his direction and realized he was watching her. Licking her dry lips, she confessed, "To tell you the truth, I am a little tired."

"The bedroom's this way, if you want to rest a bit," he said, motioning for her to follow him.

She started in the direction he indicated, but was brought up short when she spotted the huge hot tub in the corner of the room. It was a sunken one, and the surrounding walls were mirrored. Her eyes opened wider.

"It came with the room," he explained, shrugging as he lifted his eyebrows.

"Have you used it?" she asked, curiosity getting the best of her.

"Often. It's nice. Feels good to relax after a tough day," he admitted.

An image of him lying back in the hot tub, naked and wet, sent a spark of awareness through her, tightening her breasts and causing a tingling sensation between her legs.

"The bedroom's in here."

Heather was jarred from her thoughts by his voice. She slowly walked to the door and peeked inside. Spacious was an understatement. There was a large armoire, which she assumed held another television. Wide, plate-glass windows filled one whole wall. There was a door off to the right, which she suspected led to the bathroom.

And right smack-dab in the middle of a long wall was a king-size bed.

"This is your room?" she asked, and frowned at him.

Justin looked amused. "Our room," he corrected. Taking her hand, he pulled her farther inside.

Heather tugged her hand free. "What do you mean, *ours?*"

He had known this was coming, so he was prepared. "This is where we'll be sleeping."

"There isn't another bedroom?" Her questioning look challenged him.

"Sorry, honey, no."

That endearment didn't earn him any points. "Then, get me another room." It sounded like a demand. She didn't care. Stalking to the window, she looked out at the city of San Antonio, the tall buildings; the cars and people looking small and insignificant beneath them. Then she swung around to face him, her eyes flashing annoyance.

"There's no way I'm agreeing to that." He kept his tone even, not wanting to irritate her any more than he already had. "We can't work on our marriage if we're not living together."

Heather stared at him, her temper simmering. She hated that his reasoning made sense. "Justin, you promised—"

"No sex," he interrupted, not looking at all happy about it. "You didn't say anything about not sleeping together."

"You *knew* that's what I meant!"

His lips turned up in an engaging smile, flashing his dimple. "No, you said *exactly* what you meant. No sex. I agreed to that. Now I'm asking you to honor our agreement, as well."

She looked as if steam were going to rise out of her at any moment. He approached her and stopped just short of touching her. "I promised not to make love to you, and I won't, until you're ready. But I intend to sleep in that bed with you. Every single night for the next two weeks."

Until you're ready.

Frustration swept through her as his words reverberated in her mind. He was essentially telling her they *would* be making love; it was only a matter of time. Well, what had she thought? That she'd come to Texas with him and nothing would happen? Well, maybe she *had* known they'd end up making love at some point, and she had to admit to herself that her attraction to her husband grew every moment they were together. If she were honest, she'd have to confess that she missed making love with him also. Justin had been an exciting and demanding lover, arousing her in ways she'd never known possible.

But sleeping together? She *hadn't* thought they'd be sleeping together. Not this soon. Not tonight!

Glaring at him, she crossed her arms over her chest. "I want the side by the window."

Justin's grin was easy and agreeable. "You've got it." Even pouting, she was beautiful. "Now that we have that settled, do you want to get something to eat?" He figured he'd opt for food rather than ravish his wife, which was all he'd been able to think about since they'd walked into the suite.

"I'd rather take a short nap," she admitted. "I don't know why I'm so tired."

Putting his arm around her, he led her toward the bed. "Go ahead and rest. I've got some work to take care of. When you wake up, we'll have a nice dinner somewhere." He started to let her go, but he just couldn't. Wrapping his arms around her, he hugged her to him. As he rested his cheek along the side of her head, he inhaled the rose-sweet scent of her. "I'm glad you're here," he whispered huskily.

Heather felt her entire body go weak. It was so good to be held by him. He had a tender side she'd rarely seen during their marriage, but to her surprise and fascination, he'd given her several glimpses of it since he'd walked back into her life.

She put her arms around his waist and hugged him close, and his warmth surrounded her. At that moment, she thought of how wonderful it would be to stay in his arms, to lift her face and taste his mouth on hers. His hand caressed her hair, then slid down the length of her spine, leaving heat and awareness in its wake. Heather automatically pressed closer.

''Heather.''

She lifted her head, bringing her mouth near his. His breath tickled her lips, which parted in anticipation of his kiss. It was only a fraction of a second before he lowered his mouth.

A loud knock on the door stilled his movements. Justin stared at Heather—the trace of desire in her eyes, her sensuous lips, the tiny throb of her pulse at the base of her neck.

''Damn,'' he muttered. ''It's probably our luggage.'' He didn't release her.

''Probably.'' She dropped her arms, freeing him to move.

The knock came again.

Justin kissed her mouth briefly, cursed under his breath and let her go. ''Damn poor timing,'' he muttered. Stopping at the door, he turned to face her. ''Go ahead and get some rest.'' Then he was gone.

Heather smiled to herself, not even sure relaxing was even possible now. She was tingling all over. Sitting on the edge of the bed, she slipped off her sandals, then dug her toes into the plush beige carpet beneath her feet. Looking around her, she fell back on the bed, bracing herself with her elbows.

She heard Justin talking to bellman, then heard the door close. Her heart thumped, and she realized she was waiting to see if he would come back and pick up where he'd left off. But he didn't.

And despite her decision not to make love with him, she couldn't help feeling disappointed instead of relieved.

Justin set his laptop on the desk near the window, but his thoughts were not on his work. He breathed deeply and exhaled, trying to bring his libido under control. He'd accomplished one goal—getting Heather to come to Texas with him. A sigh of satisfaction escaped his lips as he flipped open the laptop and hit the power button.

That she lay sleeping in his bed played havoc with his emotions. He wanted nothing more than to join her there and tease her with slow kisses and warm caresses. His body throbbed from thoughts of making love to her. It was agony thinking about how long it had been since he'd touched her.

But he had given her his word, and even if it killed him, he'd keep it.

He glanced toward the bedroom as he hit a button for his e-mail. Anticipation filled him as she slept. They'd only just arrived, and he couldn't get enough of her. Unable to sit and work, Justin got up and stretched. He turned off his computer, sat on the sofa and switched on the television, keeping the volume low so as not to wake her.

He was tempted to go in and lay beside her, but wasn't sure if it would be a good move on his part. She'd agreed to stay after realizing they'd be sleeping together, and he didn't want to push his luck. He wanted her to feel comfortable with him. He knew it was going to take time.

The problem was, he only had *two weeks*.

Heather opened her eyes and felt disoriented as she took in her strange surroundings. Finally her mind cleared, and she realized where she was.

With Justin. In Texas. Without Timmy.

Timmy!

She'd meant to call her mother upon her arrival. How could she have forgotten? Ah, yes, she thought, her skin tingling. Being held by Justin had apparently distracted her.

Sitting up quickly, she jumped off the bed and padded barefoot across the room to the door. Her gaze searched the sitting area of the suite for Justin, then she spotted him lying on his back on the small sofa. He was asleep, his face resting against one of the floral-patterned throw pillows. He had removed his sport coat. One of his legs dangled off the end of the sofa, the other rested on the floor.

She smiled at the adorable picture he made. Then she laughed at herself. She'd never before used the term *adorable* to describe Justin. Driven, distant, powerful, sometimes even formidable, but never *adorable*. She quietly closed the door to the bedroom, then hurried to the nightstand. After glancing over the instructions for making a long distance call, she punched in the telephone number to her house.

Kathryn answered on the third ring, and they chatted for a few minutes. Heather was relieved to hear that Timmy was doing fine. Still, her chest tightened as they talked. Just knowing her mother was holding Timmy made her want to cry. Tears slid down her cheeks when she heard her son begin to fret in the background. By the time she hung up the telephone, she was a nervous wreck.

Shaking, she went into the bathroom to wash her face. She stopped as she entered, and stared. The large room was beautifully tiled in warm beige and blue. Gold fixtures accented the sink, as well as the enormous tub. Debating taking a bath, she went back into the bedroom and carefully opened the door leading to the living area. Justin was still asleep. Quietly, she walked over and retrieved her suitcases.

She went back into the bedroom and deposited the bags on the bed. Popping one open, she selected something to wear, then went into the bathroom to draw warm water into the tub. As it filled, she removed her clothes and stepped in, then lowered herself into the water as she pushed a button to start the jets.

Heather sighed as she leaned back and rested, letting the water ease the tension in her body. Justin hadn't said what their plans were for the evening, but knowing him, he'd already decided where and what they'd be doing. She turned off the water. Her nap had helped to restore her energy, but did little to relieve her inner turmoil. She tried to relax as she began to bathe.

Maybe she never should have agreed to two weeks with Justin. Maybe she should have told him about Timmy.

Don't go getting cold feet.

Okay, she'd stick with her plan, she decided, for a while longer. She finished her bath, combed out her hair and put on light makeup. Then she donned a green dress that brought out the emerald color in her eyes. She struggled for a moment with the zipper, then blew out a exasperated breath. A knock on the door stilled her movements.

"Heather?" Justin's voice was followed by another couple of taps.

Crossing to the door, she opened it. "Hi. I took a bath while you were sleeping."

"I wasn't sure if I was intruding." He leaned against the doorjamb and looked at her. Her face was flushed, and her skin glowing. His body tightened as her unique scent drifted to him.

"Of course not."

"I heard you in the bath. Was everything all right? Is there anything you need?"

She shook her head. "No. That tub in there is lethal though." His lips curved into a little smile that made her look quickly away. "I didn't want to get out."

His nostrils flared. The thought of her lying naked in warm sudsy water was almost more than Justin could stand. His appreciative gaze swept slowly over her. "You look lovely."

"Thank you," she said, and blushed with pleasure. "Um, would you mind?" She turned her back and lifted her hair. "I, uh, couldn't quite reach this."

"Not at all." Justin moved into the room and stopped behind her. He slipped the zipper up, then slid his hands over her shoulders and rested them against her neck. Leaning down, he kissed her there, briefly, and felt a charge of awareness spark between them. Her head tilted slightly.

"Thank you," she whispered huskily, then turned to face him.

He winked. "You're welcome."

She stepped slightly away, feeling a tingle of pleasure where his lips had touched her skin. She had to prevent herself from lifting her hand to the spot. "What are our plans for tonight? I wasn't sure how to dress."

"I thought we'd have dinner at the Tower Restaurant. It's a revolving restaurant that overlooks the city."

She looked as if she didn't believe him. "Really?"

"I promise."

She smiled up at him. *Another promise.* "It sounds lovely. Since I don't know anything about the city, I'm in your hands."

Justin wished that were true. He wanted his hands all over her. He settled for kissing her briefly on the lips.

Much later, they were enjoying dinner at the restaurant Justin had described. It did indeed turn in a very slow circle so as to give them a view of the city from all angles. Heather stared out the large plate-glass window at the city night scene. Justin hadn't been kidding when he described the view. It was magical. Lights glistened all over HemisFare Park, which had been built for the Texas World's Fair in the sixties and was now a central point of the downtown area.

"It's truly beautiful."

Justin grinned briefly. "I thought you'd like it."

Heather studied him, as he turned his head and looked at the view. Since they'd been together, neither had brought up anything about their separation or the problems of their marriage. She wasn't sure why Justin hadn't talked about it, other than that he wasn't one to delve into his personal feelings. Anything she'd gotten out of him while they'd lived together had had to be dragged out of him.

She hadn't brought up the subject because she was reluctant to change the easy mood between them. But she knew the longer they waited, the harder it would be. They were going to have to discuss what went wrong in order to be sure things didn't go sour again.

Still, as the evening passed, they made small talk. Justin told her a little more about the Fortunes. She learned that he and Emma weren't the only lost heirs of the family. Miranda's brother, Cameron, had fathered three illegitimate children. So far, they'd all been located, but his daughter, Holly Douglas, hadn't seen fit to return their letters.

"She lives in a remote town in the Alaskan wilderness." Justin took a bite of his smoked pork tenderloin.

"I wonder why she doesn't answer the letters?" Heather replied thoughtfully. "Surely she must be curious."

"No telling."

"What about Cameron's sons?" She wondered if she'd meet them.

"Storm Pierce is a gunnery sergeant and Jonas Goodfellow is an international importer, I believe."

"You have quite a family, Justin," she commented. She chewed and swallowed a piece of grilled asparagus. "I don't think I can keep everyone straight."

"You probably won't meet everyone on this trip. I'm not sure what Gabrielle's and Emma's plans are. By the way, I called Miranda. If it's all right, I'd like to take you to meet her tomorrow."

Heather swallowed hard, and the food in her mouth

lodged somewhere between her throat and her stomach. She wasn't sure she was prepared for meeting *any* of the new people in his life yet. At the moment, *they* seemed more a part of him than *she* did. She tried to tamp down her uneasiness. "Of course. That's why we're here."

His eyes darkened with something akin to fury. "Heather, that's not the only reason you're here with me, and you know it."

Red blotches stained her cheeks. His whole demeanor changed—from the way he sat back stiffly in his chair, to the tightening of his jaw. "Well, of course, I know—"

"Is that why you came with me?" he demanded, his tone filled with suspicion. "Just to meet the Fortunes?"

"No. Of course not." She was surprised by his fervent reaction. "It's just that we haven't really talked about *us,* about what happened."

His shoulders relaxed, and he leaned toward her, focusing his attention on her eyes. "I'm sorry. I've thought about this a lot, and I think we should spend a day or so just being together, getting used to each other again. Let's not force it, okay?"

Nodding, she said, "All right." Maybe he was right, but Heather knew there was so much more for her to think about, to stress over.

Seven

Instead of going straight back to their hotel, Justin took his time and drove around the city of San Antonio, pointing to several interesting sites, including the Alamodome, where sports events were played. He also drove by the Alamo and promised he'd take Heather there tomorrow.

When he'd said the word *promise,* she'd looked at him, and they'd shared a smile—they both knew the meaning underlying the word. A companionable silence fell over them as they arrived back at their suite.

"Would you like something to drink?" he asked, indicating the wet bar in the corner of the room.

She shook her head, and auburn curls danced around her face. "Oh, no. I'm still full from dinner. That was so nice." Her deep-green eyes shone with pleasure.

Justin was pleased she'd enjoyed herself. He

walked over to her and drew her against him, rubbing her shoulders with his hands. She stiffened slightly, but didn't pull away, and just having his arms around her felt like a victory.

"It's been quite a day. Are you tired?"

"Very," she admitted. "What I really want is to get out of these heels."

He playfully wriggled his eyebrows and gave her a devious grin. "I can help with that." She gave a squeal, as he dipped and swiftly lifted her in his arms.

"Justin!" she screamed as she clasped her hands around his neck.

Chuckling, he walked into their bedroom and sat on the bed, keeping her in his lap. He removed first one heel, then the other. She was still holding onto him.

He looked at her then, and his expression turned serious. "Ah, sweetheart, I've missed you," he murmured, and he nuzzled her neck with his cheek.

"Justin." His name came out as just a whisper from her lips.

"Hmm?" His hand caressed her back, then slid into her hair. She tilted her head as his lips explored her skin. "I love the way you smell," he whispered. Just like he remembered, like delicate roses. Her scent enveloped him, playing with his senses.

His lips explored her neck, then her chin. He kissed his way to her mouth, then stopped before taking it. Lifting his head, he looked deeply into her eyes. She didn't have to say anything. Desire flamed in her pupils, and he just about came undone. He touched her mouth briefly with his thumb. "Only a kiss," he whispered, holding her gaze captive.

He waited a millisecond for her to protest, then

lowered his mouth and took hers in an achingly hungry kiss, devouring her lips. Wriggling in his arms, she made a tiny sound of surrender. Justin felt his heartbeat take off like a rocket, sending his control into a spin. He slid both hands behind her head, and held her face still. Time ceased to exist as he ravished her lips, tasting her, remembering when he'd had the right to kiss her at will, to make love to her without thinking about anything but the erotic pleasure he could give her.

You gave up that right when you walked away.

The thought hit him like a cold splash of water in the face. He fought to regain control, then he lifted his mouth and leaned his forehead against hers. His breathing was ragged, and it was a few moments before he tried to speak.

"Damn."

Heather heaved a deep, agonizing breath. "What?"

Justin lifted her from his lap and set her on her feet. "I've got to quit making you promises," he muttered gruffly, then looked at her, his features strained. "Why don't you get ready for bed?" It came out as a question, but his crisp tone made her back away.

He needed some time alone. He was hard and ready for her, wanting nothing more than to strip her clothes from her body and make love to her—the hot, fiery, lusty kind that filled his soul.

Heather quickly gathered her clothing, then went into the bathroom and closed the door. He heard the water running and breathed hard. It had taken every ounce of his self-control to stop kissing her. How the hell was he going to get through the night sleeping with her?

He heard her moving around in the bathroom, then

the doorknob as she turned it and opened the door. She was covered in a lavender silk robe that molded her lush curves and seductively tormented him. A knot formed in his gut.

"All yours," she said quietly, avoiding his eyes, then she turned her back and put some of her clothing away.

Justin escaped inside the bathroom for a cold shower. It served its purpose, cooling his skin and easing the pain in his lower anatomy. Barely. He turned the water off, dried, then pulled on some dark blue briefs in deference to their peculiar circumstances. When he opened the bathroom door, his heated gaze immediately swept the room for her.

She was lying in the bed, the covers pulled over her body. Her hair looked soft and shiny against the stark white sheets. Hardly making a sound, Justin walked over to the edge of the bed. He switched off the light, then climbed in beside her. Moonlight shone through the gauzy curtains, bathing them with just enough light for him to see her. Rolling on his side toward her, he reached over and stroked the length of her arm with his palm.

"Come here."

She rolled a fraction toward him. Her eyes were wary, her expression questioning, yet she said nothing.

"I just want to hold you. I need to sleep with you in my arms." He reached for her, and she scooted back toward him, then faced away again. He moved closer, spooning her with his body. She was soft and warm, and he slipped his arm around her, tugging her more tightly against him.

"Are you comfortable?"

Heather sighed as his heat enveloped her. "Yes," she said softly. But she wasn't. All she could think about was the way he'd kissed her, and how deliciously wonderful it felt to be held by him.

He nuzzled her neck. "I want you to know something," he whispered in the darkness.

"Hmm?" Heather murmured dreamily. She touched his hand where it rested on her belly, then wrapped hers around it. A closeness they'd never before shared enshrouded them.

"There's never been anyone else."

Heather's breath caught. She hadn't wanted to think about Justin's life without her, so she'd purposely put it out of her mind. Now, he was telling her he hadn't been with another woman in the year they'd been separated.

"Justin—"

His light kiss on her neck interrupted her. "Shh. I just wanted you to know, I've never wanted anyone but you."

Heather tucked his candid declaration in her heart. Until now, though she wanted their marriage to work, she hadn't truly let herself believe it would. For the very first time, she felt hope.

Heather walked into the living area of the hotel suite from the bedroom. She'd chosen another sundress to wear—this one red, with tiny white polkadots. Not knowing exactly what to expect, she didn't want to be overdressed or underdressed to meet Miranda Fortune. She wanted to look perfect.

Justin's gaze traveled appreciatively over her as she came farther into the room. She shivered, feeling as if he'd touched her. Her eyes widened as she looked at him. He was dressed in a suit, which really didn't surprise her. It struck her that one thing about him that hadn't changed was the fact that he still didn't have the slightest idea what it meant to relax. The entire time they'd been married, she'd never seen him in jeans and a T-shirt. He'd occasionally worn sweats, but only while exercising. Casual clothing to Justin usually meant wearing khaki pants and a printed, button-down shirt.

"I think I'm underdressed," she commented, nodding at his clothes.

"You look wonderful," Justin replied. "Good enough to eat." His lips turned up slightly as he strolled toward her.

"But you're dressed more formally. I should have thought—"

"Don't change. I want you to be yourself. You don't have to dress or act a certain way to meet Miranda." He briefly kissed her, tasting her lips, then reluctantly pulled away.

"If you're sure." Heather sucked in a rigid breath. Justin had been kissing her more and more, and she felt a thrill of excitement every time he touched her. The sexual tension between them was growing, and she wasn't sure what to do about it. She wasn't ready to resume that part of their marriage—not until they worked through what had happened to them in the past.

But it was so hard not to give in to the desire growing moment by moment inside her.

Though she was still uncomfortable with her choice of clothing, Justin again reassured her she looked beautiful. Heather finally trusted him on that, and they left the hotel. A few minutes later they were heading toward Miranda's house.

"Oh, my," Heather exclaimed, blinking with surprise, as Justin drove up to his mother's home in his rental car. "This is absolutely beautiful." She gazed with wonder at the large Mediterranean-style villa surrounded by lush native plants. Miranda's home in the lavish community of Kingston Estates was everything he'd told her and more. Getting used to the wealth Justin had personally acquired had taken some time. Seeing the extent of the affluence of the Fortunes...well, Heather was striving hard not to gape. Obviously, they were rich beyond any capability of her imagination.

"She's just a person," Justin assured her, then got out and walked around the car. He opened her door, then offered his hand for support.

"She's your mother."

He nodded. "That, too."

"Can I change my mind?"

Justin favored her with a crooked smile. "Not on your life."

An edginess Justin hadn't anticipated tugged at him as he led her up the walk. As he'd told Heather, Miranda had asked to meet her. That request had surprised him. He supposed it was natural for Miranda to want to meet her daughter-in-law, especially since he hadn't been up-front about their separation. He just hadn't been able to admit that his marriage to Heather was in trouble, that they had been living apart, that he hadn't seen her in a year.

Now he was feeling foolish for not being totally open about his and Heather's relationship. Despite his resolve to remain aloof with the Fortune clan, Justin was finding it more and more difficult to keep them at a distance. He found himself looking forward to each trip he took to Texas—this one in particular.

He *wanted* Heather to like Miranda. He knew Miranda would love her.

Heather's gaze drifted over the spacious stucco structure. Justin took her hand. "You okay?" She gave him a wan smile, as they approached the door.

Apparently, Miranda had been watching for them. The door opened, and Miranda's gaze lit up with excitement when she greeted them. The wall around his heart took another blow.

"Hello, Justin," she said, and smiled widely.

"Miranda." Justin's lips lifted briefly.

"And you must be Heather." Miranda extended her hand, her gaze fairly bubbling with warmth and enthusiasm, as if she'd known Heather for years and was an old friend she hadn't seen in a while.

"Yes." Heather nodded and shook her hand, then unconsciously stepped closer to Justin.

"I'm so happy to meet you." She opened the door wider and stepped aside, allowing them to enter.

Heather's sandals clicked as they met the imported tile floor. Miranda Fortune, as it turned out, was nothing like what she had imagined. As she had guessed, Justin's mother *was* beautiful. Elegantly dressed, her presence upon entering a room would demand the attention of those already present. Though Heather often felt people with the kind of money these people had were pretentious, and often snobby, she was pleasantly surprised to find Miranda cordial and welcoming.

"Thank you." She took note of her surroundings,

hoping her fascination wasn't too apparent. "Your home is very lovely."

"Thank you so much. Please come in."

They followed her through the house to the sunroom, where Justin sat on the sofa, and Heather took a seat beside him. He put his arm around her shoulders, drawing her closer.

Sitting down, Miranda said, "I'm so glad you brought Heather to meet me."

Heather was mesmerized by the woman's rather striking blue eyes. They were identical to that of her son's. If ever there was a doubt of his parentage, those clear, intense, beautiful blue eyes destroyed it.

Miranda turned her attention to Heather. "Justin told me that you're a school teacher," she commented. "What grade do you teach?"

"First."

"I'm sure that it's very rewarding."

"It is, most of the time. I love it. The children are so adorable and very anxious to learn."

"It's a very time-consuming job, I'm sure."

Heather nodded. She thought of Timmy and how demanding her job had become once she had him. "It gets crazy at times," she admitted.

Miranda looked at her son. "Well, I hope you'll be able to enjoy some of San Antonio while you're here. How long are you planning on staying?"

"About two weeks," Justin answered. He looked at Heather, and she nodded.

"That's wonderful." Miranda sat forward, hesitated, then said, "I know this is short notice, but I wasn't sure if you'd be here so I didn't mention it before. I'm involved with a local charity, and we're having a gala tomorrow evening to raise money for it. There'll be dinner and dancing. I would really love it if you could come.''

Heather could tell this was something important to Miranda. She looked at Justin, but he remained silent. "What kind of charity is it?" she asked.

"It's for an organization called Teen House. They provide guidance and a place to live for pregnant teens." She frowned, and remorse filled her gaze, coloring her skin slightly pink. "I'm sure Justin has told you of the circumstances of his birth." He nodded, and his lips thinned slightly. Miranda took a breath. "I'm not proud of giving up my children, but at the time, I thought I was doing what was best for them."

Heather felt Justin tense beside her. "I'm sure you did," she replied, understanding how difficult a decision it must have been for Miranda. Still, her loyalty was to Justin.

Miranda gave her son a deep apologetic look. "I can't undo the past, as much as I wish I could."

He nodded. "I know that." He didn't like talking about the past. It wouldn't change anything. The future was another story.

"I feel that by working with this organization, I'm helping to prevent other young women from making a mistake they, too, might later regret."

Justin squeezed Heather's shoulder, but he said nothing. "That's very admirable, Mrs. Fortune," she said.

"Please, call me Miranda."

Heather turned her head toward Justin so she could look into his eyes. "Would you like to go?"

His composed expression didn't change. "I'll leave it up to you."

"You don't have to give me an answer now," Miranda assured them.

"I think I'd love an evening of dancing," Heather replied, hoping she was making the right decision. Still aware of the tenseness in Justin, she was pleased when Miranda's facial muscles relaxed. "Thank you so much for asking us."

"Hopefully, you'll get a chance to meet some of Justin's family, too."

"I'm looking forward to it."

They talked for a few more minutes, then left, assuring Miranda that they'd see her the next evening. Though Justin wasn't totally at ease the entire time they were visiting Miranda, it was evident to Heather that he had accepted her as his biological mother, and as such, gave her the respect one would give a parent. Already it was easy to see that he now regarded her as much more than a short-term presence in his life.

Secretly, she had expected to be pumped for information about Justin and about their relationship during their visit. However, Miranda seemed to respect their privacy, and Heather actually liked her. She saw sadness in Miranda's eyes when she looked at her son. Her opinion of her husband's mother rose a notch.

Justin opened the car door for her, and she got inside. When he didn't close it immediately, she glanced up expectantly at him. Her heart thudded as he leaned down toward her. Her lips parted as he kissed her mouth, and she sighed with pleasure from the taste of him.

But all too quickly he drew away, and she was left feeling deprived of gratification, as he got behind the wheel. She looked at him as he started the engine and drove away.

"Your mother is very nice."

He took her hand and squeezed it, then let it go. "It meant a lot to her that you took the time to come and meet her. I wish you could have met Emma and Flynn. And Rose. She's adorable."

Heather's heart squeezed at the mention of Emma's baby. "Me, too."

Justin didn't miss the flicker of anguish that passed through her eyes before she could conceal it, and he regretted bringing up Emma's baby. He didn't want to hurt her. As he looked back at the road, he was sure she was thinking about her miscarriage. Frustration pulled at him. He wanted to ease her pain, but had no idea how to go about it.

He still felt the same agonizing pain when he thought of the baby they'd lost. Maybe together they could find a way to get past it. If they could rebuild their life together, they could try to have another child. He chanced a glanced at her, and prudently decided not to broach the subject yet. But he *was* going to. It was just a matter of time.

"What do you think about the organization your mother is involved in?" she asked, breaking into his thoughts.

Justin wrinkled his brows and shrugged indifferently. "It's a worthy cause."

"And that's all you think about it?" His words were carefully chosen. Part of their problems had stemmed from their inability to communicate. Maybe they couldn't talk about their personal feelings just yet, but she saw this as an opportunity to get him to open up a bit.

He gave her a curious look. "What exactly do you want me to say?"

"What you really feel."

He shifted uncomfortably in his seat and shrugged again. "I just told you—"

"Come on, just think about it." Heather scooted closer to him. She touched the back of his neck with her fingers. "It must have taken a lot of courage for her to get involved with an agency like that."

Apparently Justin was following her drift, but it was obvious he wasn't sure what she expected of him. His idea of handling the past was probably putting it behind him and not talking about it.

"I'm sure it did."

Realizing she was not gaining much ground, Heather sighed. "You know, she's not proud of what she did. She truly thought she was doing what was best for you and Emma."

Justin stretched his shoulders as he maneuvered in the traffic. "I know."

Heather ran her hand along his arm. "Just think about what she must have been going through. She was so young. Maybe she felt she had no one to turn to." Resting her palm against his cheek, she said softly, "I know it still hurts."

He put his hand over hers, and glanced briefly at her, his own eyes haunted. "Nothing hurts as much as losing you."

"Oh, Justin." Heather's heart melted. In his eyes she saw sorrow and regret. She realized that he meant it, that no matter what had happened in the past, he truly wanted her back in his life. She prayed they could make up for lost time, for all the mistakes they had made.

Small steps.

At least today they'd taken a few.

They spent the afternoon sightseeing. While in San Antonio alone, Justin hadn't had much inclination to tour the notable sites, but he enjoyed exploring them with Heather. After driving along Mission Trail, they visited one of the famous historic missions, then went on to Alamo Plaza to see the Alamo.

Since it was nearing dinnertime by the time they left there, she suggested they head back to the hotel. When they got back, Justin entered the elevator behind her, and as soon as the door closed behind them, she felt the moving cubicle shrink from his presence. Her neck prickled as he placed his hand there, and she closed her eyes. His thumb made a circling motion along her hairline, and Heather stifled a groan of pleasure at his touch. She was losing her objectivity just by being with him. Willing herself not to move closer to him, a sigh of relief escaped her lips. The doors opened on their floor.

As they walked into their suite, Justin said, ''I thought we'd eat at one of the restaurants along the River Walk.''

''Sounds good,'' she agreed. Leaving him to check his messages, she went into the bedroom and closed the door. A few minutes later, when she came out of the bedroom, Justin was working at his computer.

''I need to do some shopping.'' Heather walked toward him as she ran a brush through her hair.

He looked up from his laptop with a mock look of amazement. ''Somehow I'm not surprised.''

She playfully threw the brush at him. With quick reflexes he deflected it, and it bounced off his arm and hit the floor. "I didn't plan on attending a charity dance," she said in her defense, coming closer. "I have nothing with me to wear."

He took her hand and tugged her close to him, then pulled her down on his lap.

"Justin!" Her squeal pierced the room as she looked up at him and giggled.

Justin suddenly sobered, then lightly kissed her lips. "It's been a long time since I've heard that." The look in his eyes made her still. "I've missed hearing you laugh." He touched her cheek with his finger. "I've missed a lot about you, Heather. It's been one hell of a long year without you."

His confession warmed her heart, and his arms around her set her body on fire. "I've missed you, too." However much she wanted to remain distant, even for just a while longer, she couldn't deny him this truth. "I truly have."

"Do you mean that?" he asked, his gaze holding hers.

"Yes," she whispered, yet there was a hesitancy in her voice.

"But?"

"I don't want to rush into anything."

To Justin's way of thinking, if they took it any slower, he'd die from wanting her. "I won't rush you," he promised, kissing her lips. "But I'm going to have a good time convincing you."

Eight

Heather leaned in to Justin, giving herself up to the pleasure of his kiss. Reluctantly, she pulled away. "Uh, shopping, remember?" she said, feeling disoriented from the desire spinning through her.

He tapped her nose with a light kiss. "Before or after dinner?"

"Before," she said decisively, aware that he'd let her make the choice.

They spent the next couple of hours going from store to store at the River Walk Mall, sharing an easy rapport, touching each other, flirting a little, and enjoying being in each other's company. Heather felt encouraged. He'd had done everything in his power so far to make their reconciliation as smooth as possible. Still, there were things they needed to iron out that they seemed to be avoiding. It was always on her mind.

After trying on several gowns, each of which met with Justin's approval, she ended up choosing an emerald green, when Justin told her it was his favorite choice because it brought out the color of her eyes.

When they'd finished shopping for her, Heather suggested they pick out some clothes for him. Justin balked at first, but she was insistent.

"I'd love to see your buns in a pair of jeans," she told him, and sent him a seductive smile.

"Damn," Justin muttered, accepting defeat. "I've never cared much for them, but how can I disappoint you?"

Later that night after dinner, they decided to stroll along the cobblestone walkways. The chatter of tourists and locals laughing and talking filled the air around them. They paused as they crossed over one of the arched bridges to watch a boat go by on the San Antonio River. Nearby, a baby squealed, and Heather started. At that moment, she would have given anything to have Timmy with her. Tears crested her eyes. She missed him so much! She'd used the opportunity while Justin was bathing and dressing to call her mother, but it hadn't taken away the distress of her separation from her baby. It would still be days before she could hold him and kiss him.

Justin noticed the change in her mood and reached for her hand. "Are you all right?" Silently, she nodded, and he quietly said, "Honey, we can have another baby."

"I know." She realized he thought her sadness came from thinking about the baby they'd lost. "It's just that—"

"We could start all over again, Heather. Start another family, get back what we used to have—if you'd just give us a chance.''

''I'm trying,'' she told him, flooded with guilt. She was so very tempted to tell him then, to get it over with. But he pulled her to him, and every thought left her mind as she rested her head on his shoulder, letting him end the war within her, without ever being aware of doing so. They stood silently in each other's arms as he stroked her head, and the world around them disappeared when he lifted her face and pressed his lips on hers.

There was an unspoken promise in his kiss, in the gentle yet restrained way he held her to him. She could feel the tension mount between them, the power of his kiss slowly, provocatively tearing down the barriers she'd built around her heart.

She wasn't used to losing control, had used hurt and pain to keep the barriers up for so long that she was taken aback by how easily he was able to ravage her senses. It was getting harder to keep him at bay because she wanted her husband in the most intimate of ways.

When she suggested going back to their suite, Justin readily agreed. Once there, she readied herself for bed, aware more than ever of the sexual tension building between them, her body still on fire, her desire for her husband a burning, aching need.

But old doubts began to plague her as she climbed into bed. Moments later, Justin joined her and pulled her into his arms. He kissed her hungrily, and Heather gave herself up to the moment, tamping down her reservations, wanting him inside her.

''Ah, Heather.'' Justin ran his hand along her rib cage to her breast, caressing her through the thin silk of her gown. His fingers toyed with the bud of her nipple, and she sighed pleasurably. Her hips pressed against him as his mouth claimed hers again. "I want you back as my wife. Now." He rained kisses along her chin and neck, then lower, edging her gown up over her belly to bare her breasts. He kissed one, then the other, his tongue leaving a slick wet trail along her skin.

"Justin." Heather writhed beneath him, her senses swirling. "Oh," she murmured between clenched teeth as he covered her nipple with his mouth and sucked her hard.

"Say you want me, too." He shoved her night-gown up over her head, then pinned her arms above her. Her back arched, lifting her to him. He groaned low in his throat as he pleasured her, building the intensity inside her body.

Her hips moved as his mouth moved lower, kissing her belly, then lower still, his tongue wet and warm. He slipped his hands beneath her hips, clutching her bottom.

"Tell me you want me to love you," he demanded, his voice husky with need.

Love.

"Wait." Stiffening, she came up on her elbows as she drew her legs up. What was she doing? Could she go through with this, reestablish this part of their relationship, without knowing if Justin truly loved her? If there truly was enough love between them to make their marriage work?

Startled by her abrupt withdrawal, Justin stared at her. She was barely able to make out his features in the darkness, but she noticed the tightening of his jaw line and heard his quick intake of breath.

"Heather?"

"I'm sorry. I thought I was ready for this, but I'm not." She scooted farther away, distancing herself physically, as she'd done mentally. Her desire for sexual fulfillment had temporarily confused her, clouding her thoughts. Her breasts were full, aching for his touch, and she stared at him, her cheeks burning with embarrassment as she hurriedly put her gown back on.

She'd gotten carried away. He was probably furious with her, and rightly so. But how could she explain to him that desire couldn't replace love? She wanted to believe that he loved her, but he'd said nothing to relieve her fears that this could all be a mistake. Everything had happened so fast, had blindsided her. "I'm sorry," she blurted again, her voice cracking. "I didn't mean to lead you on."

Justin groaned, then rolled on his back, his breathing labored. He rubbed his face wearily, willing his body to calm down. Hell, he'd told her he wouldn't rush her. He'd actually *promised* he wouldn't.

"Justin?"

"What?" It came out gruff. His body was still screaming for release, and it was going to take him a few minutes to get total control. Or some privacy.

"I really am sorry."

"I know."

For a while, neither spoke. A few minutes later, when he felt more in power of his body, he rolled toward her. She hadn't moved, was still sitting in a tight ball, staring at him and looking frightened.

"Come here," he said, his voice still a little raw. She didn't move. "Come on," repeated, this time a little more gently. She slowly straightened her legs and edged down on the bed beside him. He drew her against him, settling her backside against his thighs.

He kissed her neck, then murmured, "It's okay." But frustration was still evident in his tone. "Look at me."

She twisted her head in his direction.

"Sweetheart, I want to make love to you," he said evenly. "As you can easily tell, more than anything, I want to be inside you. But when we make love, it will be a commitment to our marriage. Once I have you," he whispered huskily, "I'll never let you go again." He kissed her mouth, then rolled on his back, maneuvering her body and taking her with him. Her leg intimately straddled his as she snuggled next to his chest. "And that's a promise."

They were startled awake early the next morning by the telephone. Justin answered it on the second ring. He talked quietly, not wanting to disturb Heather, but when he glanced back at her she was already sitting up in bed. After a few minutes, he hung up the phone and looked at her, his expression pasty white.

"That was Miranda. Her brother Ryan is ill," he explained.

"What is it?" she asked, her heart thudding. The first person she'd thought about when the phone rang was Timmy. Relief washed over her, even as she began to feel concerned about Justin's uncle.

"They don't know yet."

"Has he been hospitalized?"

Justin shook his head. "No, but he's under a doctor's care."

Heather rubbed the sleep from her eyes, then ran a hand through her tangled hair. "Do you want to go to see him?"

Justin's expression lifted a bit. "Would you mind? This is supposed to be our time together."

She touched his cheek. "Of course not. They're your family."

They are my family. Justin thought about it as he went into the bathroom to shower. He was beginning to care deeply for them, especially Miranda. Now, he reasoned, if he could only reach Heather, his life would be almost perfect.

As he came out of the bathroom, she was hanging up the telephone. "Everything all right?"

"Yes. I just like to keep in touch with Mom," she explained.

Justin nodded. "Sure. I imagine she's concerned about you." Heather and her mother were close, and he'd sometimes envied their relationship.

"I won't be long," she assured him, watching him pull a blue suit from the closet.

"Why don't you wear the jeans and shirt we bought yesterday?"

His brow lifted as he considered her suggestion. The idea of wearing the jeans still seemed foreign to him.

"Come on. They'll look great." Her tone was convincing.

Finally he nodded, and she disappeared into the bathroom. When she came out of the bedroom a while later, Justin was leaning over his computer. Heather took one look at his backside, and desire coursed through her.

"Maybe I shouldn't have talked you into those

jeans," she said, appreciating the way they hugged his hips and muscular thighs. Heavens! Though she'd guessed he'd look good in a pair of jeans, she'd never expected that admiring him would turn her on. She'd created her own kind of torture. Walking over to him, she put her arms around his waist and hugged him from behind.

"If I'd thought even for a minute that they'd cause this kind of reaction with you," he stated, "I'd have worn them a long time ago." He turned in her arms and gave her a seductive look.

She lifted her lips for his kiss as she cupped his bottom. "You're too sexy for your own good," she complained, teasing him with a wink.

"Keep that up and we're never going to get out of here," he warned her. He kissed her hard, then set her away from him.

He picked up his keys and walked to the door, leaving her with an incredible sense of longing.

They arrived at the Double Crown Ranch in Red Rock about mid-morning. Having thought it wasn't possible to be any more impressed by the wealth of the Fortunes, Heather now admitted to herself that she'd been wrong. Ryan Fortune's ranch was, to say the least, imposing. She walked beside Justin toward the massive adobe house, which was surrounded by a sandstone wall. They passed through the arched entryway and followed a curving stone walkway toward the house.

Despite her decision to accompany Justin, Heather felt a bit nervous about meeting more of his family. Being introduced one-on-one to Miranda had been easy compared to the idea of encountering the Fortune family on a moment's notice. As they approached, the antique wooden door opened and Miranda greeted them. Miranda hugged Heather and then Justin, who surprised Heather by allowing his mother to do so.

Other family members had also stopped by, and Heather was introduced to each of them. She wondered if she'd ever keep their names straight. Justin stayed by her side and they went to visit Ryan, who was sitting in a massive chair in the great room. His wife, Lily, stood by his side, her expression deeply worried. Justin's half brother, Kane, and his wife Allison, were also there.

Kane was talking quietly to Lily, who was listening intently. Ryan, though glad to see everyone, was clearly uncomfortable with the fuss being made over him. From the amount of attention his mysterious illness was causing, Heather surmised that he was the driving force behind the Fortune family.

Justin took her hand, and they went to talk with Kane and Ryan for a few minutes. She mostly listened as she stood by Justin's side. Ryan was quick to point out that the family was overreacting to what was clearly a lingering stomach flu, but Kane adamantly disagreed, insisting that Ryan had shown little sign of improving since he'd taken ill.

As they talked, Heather was pleased by the way the Fortunes embraced Justin as one of their own, including him in the conversation and listening intently to his opinion. His eagerness to offer his support warmed her heart. It was a side of her husband she'd been unaware of until now. While they were married, he'd always held a part of himself back. She'd never pushed him, had accepted he wouldn't allow anyone, even her, to get too close emotionally.

Until now. His acceptance of his new family showed her how much he was changing—how, little by little, he was opening up. His actions reinforced the hope she felt for the success of their reconciliation.

No doubt, they would soon be at a point in their relationship where they would be able to put past hurts away, and she would be able to tell him about his son. She prayed Justin would understand why she hadn't told him earlier.

"Who is that dancing with your mother?"

Justin tugged Heather closer to him as they moved in rhythm to a slow tune on the dimly lit dance floor. "Who cares?" he whispered, enjoying holding his wife in his arms. "My mind's on you." He nibbled at her neck, then kissed her chin.

"Justin!" Heather pulled slightly away, but only as far as his arms allowed. Her face reddened. "People are going to stare."

"I don't care," he insisted, shrugging indifferently, amusement flashing in his eyes.

"Behave!" She stretched farther away and gave him a stern look. "Now, who is that with your mother?" she repeated, touching his cheek with her hand and turning his head.

Justin's gaze swept the room of the banquet hall in the upscale hotel and settled on Miranda. He furrowed his brow as he noticed his mother in the arms of a tall, well-built man. "I don't know. I noticed her talking to him earlier."

The song ended, and Justin reluctantly let Heather go, holding her hand as they strolled back to their table. His mother arrived at the same time, escorted by her dance partner.

Justin studied the man as he stood close to Miranda, seeming reluctant to leave. His perceptive blue gaze met the man's piercing black eyes, and Justin felt a peculiar sensation in his chest.

"This is Daniel Smythe," Miranda said, introducing him. "Daniel, this is my son, Justin, and his wife, Heather.

As Justin shook Daniel's hand, the strange sensation he'd felt intensified. He studied the man as Miranda talked quietly to him, noticing that he seemed more to her than a new acquaintance. Justin was anxious to ask Miranda more about him. He got his chance after Smythe excused himself and left.

He was gone only a second before Justin asked, almost demanded, to know what Miranda knew about him.

Looking a bit startled, she replied, "I know he's a successful businessman in the oil industry."

He frowned at his mother. "Did you just meet him here tonight?" he asked, casting her a curious glance, suddenly aware of his protective feelings for her. To him, the two of them seemed awfully friendly to have just met.

"Um, no," Miranda admitted, and she chewed at her bottom lip.

"Then, how do you know him?" Justin stared at her. Miranda was being evasive. Who *was* this Daniel Smythe? he wondered, looking across the room and spotting the man again. Was there something she *wasn't* saying? Again, an odd feeling made his heart beat just a little harder.

"He's an old friend," she hedged, avoiding eye contact with her son.

"He's very handsome," Heather offered, glancing over at him again.

Miranda gave them a self-conscious smile. "Yes, I think so," she admitted, her expression wistful.

"How old a friend?" Justin pressed, still curious about the man.

"I knew him before you were born," Miranda reluctantly divulged. "We haven't seen each other in a very long time. He, uh, asked me out, and we're going on a date next week." A rosy flush covered her cheeks.

"A date?" Justin repeated, his voice deepening. He regarded his mother carefully. Without Kane nearby, he figured it was his duty to look after her. "Should I go over and find out his intentions?"

Both Heather and Miranda chuckled, drawing a scowl from him. "Don't you dare," Miranda pleaded, and for a moment reminded him of a schoolgirl with her first crush.

He decided there was definitely something Miranda was concealing. And it had to do with the stranger across the room. She'd admitted that she'd known him a long time ago. Justin stilled as a wild thought occurred to him.

Could Daniel Smythe be my father?

Noticing that Justin was staring intently at the man, Heather touched his arm to get his attention. "What?" she said.

Absently, he shook his head. "Nothing."

Miranda looked nervous, as if she thought he was going to embarrass her. "Heather, talk to him, please."

"I don't really have any control over him," Heather replied.

Justin gave her a purely male look. "You have more than you think," he whispered, forgetting about Miranda and Daniel Smythe as he ran an intimate gaze over his wife's body.

Their conversation was interrupted when Leeza Carter sauntered toward them. Miranda seemed to put on her socially cordial mask and turned to face her ex-husband's wife.

"Well, Miranda. Hello." She slid an curious gaze over Justin and Heather.

"Leeza." Miranda regarded the woman with obvious reserve. "How have you been doing since Lloyd's death?" She took a step closer to Justin.

"It's been difficult," Leeza replied, her expression a little too obviously sorrowful.

Justin had noticed the woman earlier in the evening when her shrill laugh drew his attention. She was dressed provocatively, her voluptuous, slightly plump figure poured into a red-sequined gown, which made him question her bereaved countenance. Not comfortable with the tension mounting between the two women, Justin put his arm around his mother.

Miranda, obligated by simple courtesy, introduced the bleached-blond woman to them. "Leeza was married to Kane's father," she explained for Heather's benefit.

Neither Justin nor Heather encouraged conversation. For lack of more to say, Leeza moved on.

Letting out a breath of relief, Miranda murmured, "I wonder why she continues to stay in San Antonio since Lloyd passed away?"

Justin continued to stare at Leeza as she walked away, then turned toward his mother. "Who knows?"

"Are you all right?" Heather asked with concern, as they took their seats.

Her features relaxing into a genuine smile, Miranda patted Heather's hand. "Yes, thank you."

Justin watched as she turned and looked at the crowd, her gaze coming to rest on Daniel Smythe. His curiosity about the man intensified.

"It's a nice turnout, isn't it?" Miranda offered.

Heather assured her it was. "I'm very impressed with the charity you're involved with," she said, wanting Miranda to know that she understood why the woman supported such a worthy cause.

Miranda tilted her head as her gaze met Justin's. "I made a terrible choice all those years ago. If I had to do it again, I would face my father's disappointment, and I would have kept you and Emma."

He placed his hand over hers without saying anything. It was his way of giving her comfort without using words. Another bit of peace filled a corner of his heart as silence settled between them.

Miranda glanced across the room again, and her brows lifted. "Is that Michelle dancing with Storm?"

Justin followed her gaze. "Michelle who?" he asked, spotting Storm Pierce across the room. In his arms was an attractive raven-haired woman.

"My friend, Michelle Guillaire. She's a wedding planner." She turned toward Heather. "I'm sorry. Has Justin told you about Storm?"

Heather searched her memory, trying to recall what connection Storm Pierce had with the family. "I think so."

"Justin's uncle, Cameron, who's deceased now,

had three illegitimate children that we also recently found out about. Along with Justin and Emma, they are also heirs of the Fortune family," she explained.

"Oh, yes, he did mention them," Heather answered, remembering the conversation she'd had with Justin about Cameron's children.

Miranda nodded, then smiled happily at them both. "I'm so glad you could come."

"We've enjoyed spending the evening with you, but I have to confess, I'm very tired." Heather sighed, then looked at Justin. It had been a long day. "I'm ready to call it a night. How about you?" she asked.

He nodded in agreement and stood, then helped her to her feet. "Thank you for inviting us, Miranda," he said.

His mother stood along with them. "Thank you for coming."

Justin leaned over and kissed her cheek.

Heather eyed the hot tub, as she and Justin entered the suite. As yet, she hadn't indulged in using it, though he had several times since she'd been there. She felt all mixed up inside and needed to relax. The idea of soaking for a few minutes was awfully tantalizing.

Justin noticed the direction of her gaze. "Why don't you get ready for bed?" he suggested.

"I think I will." She gave the hot tub another long look, then headed to the bedroom.

While Heather was changing, Justin turned on the jets to the hot tub, hoping to romance his wife and tempt her to join him. He made a quick call to room service for some wine, promising a large tip if they delivered it immediately. He found some candles in one of the drawers and lit them, setting them strategically near the mirrored walls. They gave the room a soft glow as he dimmed the lights.

Moments later, there was a soft tap at the door, and Justin accepted the wine and glasses, then gave the man from room service a hundred dollar bill.

After he poured them each a glass and placed them by the hot tub, Justin tapped on the bedroom door. Heather didn't answer, so he figured she was in the bathroom. He quickly changed his clothes. He was tempted to slip into the hot tub naked, but he didn't intend to seduce his wife tonight. When she was ready, she would come willingly to him. However, he wasn't beyond using every means at his disposal to charm her.

He was in the water when Heather walked back into the room wearing her lavender robe. Her auburn hair glowed in the flickering light of the candles, setting off its vibrant color. She looked at him with a mixture of envy and trepidation.

Justin lifted his wineglass and sipped from it. "Care to join me?"

Heather studied him. He looked so relaxed. She was tempted beyond words, but she wasn't sure about allowing herself to become vulnerable to him. Saying no to him last night had been difficult. She wasn't sure she could do it again.

The steam rising from the water beckoned to her, and she couldn't resist sharing the intimacy with him. "I'm not getting in there naked," she declared, in case he was expecting her to.

"I promise I'm not naked, sweetheart," Justin replied, though he wanted to be. He wanted them both naked. He grinned and his dimple winked at her. "Come on in."

Nine

Heather stared at him, and her control and willpower slipped another notch. She wavered for a few moments between need and sanity, and need finally won. "All right. I'll be right back," she said, giving in to the desire to soak in the hot sudsy water. She left the room and quickly changed into her bathing suit, then returned to join him, thankful he'd turned the lights down. She didn't want him to see the few tiny stretch marks on her body, a telling sign of her recent pregnancy.

Sighing appreciatively, she sank into the tub, then leaned back to relax. "Oh, my."

Justin studied her. "See what you've been missing?" he said, teasing her as his gaze slid over her shoulders, then lower where the water covered her bikini. She *looked* naked even though she wasn't. An ache began beneath his belly.

Heather stared at her husband, and the thought hit her that she'd been missing a lot. Her heart gave a jump as his seductive eyes captured hers.

"Mmm…you're right." She reached for the glass of wine he'd poured her and noticed the rose beside it. "Oh, Justin." His gesture sent a thrill through her heart.

"Remember when we first met? You always smelled like roses. I loved being near you."

Heather cocked her head at him. "That's what you remember the most about when we first met?"

He grinned mischievously. "That and wanting to get you into bed." He could see the blush rise to her face through the steam.

"You certainly didn't waste any time trying," she reminded him, her smile crooked.

"I knew you were mine. You just didn't know it."

He touched her leg with his toe, then slowly slid it up her calf. Heather's heart hammered in her chest from the sudden contact. "Yes, well, you certainly made me aware of it. I didn't stand a chance, did I?" she asked, not really expecting an answer.

"You're all I've ever wanted," Justin murmured, his voice deep. "Come here," he commanded softly.

"I don't know if that's such a good idea." Heather knew she was in trouble. A fire had started deep in the core of her. Justin slid his foot up to her thigh. She felt the fire escalate, sending shafts of need through her.

He moved a little closer. "I won't do anything you're not ready for. I promise."

There was that word again, Heather thought speculatively. He'd been making a lot of promises since he'd walked back into her life, and to his credit, he'd kept every one of them. The trouble was, she wasn't sure she could keep the promise she'd made to herself—not to become physically involved with him too soon.

Despite her reservations, she found herself moving closer. He slid his hands around her waist and lifted her to him, settling her on her knees, straddling him. Resting her rear on his muscle-hard thighs, she silently stared at him.

"It feels so good to hold you," he whispered, then he leaned forward and slowly touched his lips to hers. "To kiss you."

Heather slid her arms around his neck as his mouth took hers in a lingering, wet, seductive kiss. Her breasts tightened, her nipples hardening as they met the solid wall of his chest. Without even hesitating, she opened her mouth, and his tongue invaded it, sliding past her teeth and touching hers erotically.

Sighing with pleasure, she scooted closer to him. As he continued to kiss her, his hands slid down her back and beneath the water to cup her bottom. His finger slid beneath her bathing suit, so achingly close to the most feminine part of her that she moaned under her breath, wanting him to touch her there. Instead, in an instant his hands were on her back.

She drew away, her face only inches from his, their mouths nearly touching, their breaths intertwined. "Did you plan this?"

Justin's gaze never wavered. "What?"

"The hot tub, the candles, the wine." She hesitated, then asked, "Did you plan on sleeping with me?"

"I was hoping," he admitted, giving her the truth. He wanted her, and since she was sitting on his lap, she knew it. There was no way he could deny it. He ran his hands along her shoulders and down her arms. She felt like silk, smooth and delicate. "I want you back as my wife, Heather, and that means making love with you. But I'm not going to seduce you if that's what you're expecting."

Heather tried to swallow but couldn't. What did that mean? Before she could give it any more thought, he took her mouth in another searing kiss. When he lifted his lips, he whispered, "But you can seduce *me*. I'm perfectly willing."

His provocative suggestion gave her a visual picture of the two of them naked in each other's arms. There had been many times in the past when she'd done exactly that—seduced him. Practically naked in a thong and sexy bra, she'd met him at the door, once when he'd come home late from work. They'd made love in the hallway, unable to wait until they reached the bedroom.

Her throat closed tight, restricting her breathing, as she debated the wisdom of giving him her body when she didn't have the promise of his heart. Seeing her hesitation, he touched her skin with his tongue, sliding it between her breasts and kissing that sensitive area. And Heather wanted more, so much more. She loved him. She knew that now. And she wanted him.

Eager to relieve the frenzy of emotions controlling her body, she peeled her top off, and her breasts floated freely in the water.

Justin tested their weight in his hands, then he lifted his head and looked into her eyes. "Are you sure about this?" he asked, not wanting her to be sorry later. He wanted to make love to her with a desperate need he couldn't even understand, but not at the risk of losing her.

"I'm sure," she whispered. "I've missed being with you."

Justin lifted one of her breasts to his mouth. "Have you missed this?" As he gently sucked on her nipple, he shifted his gaze to her face. Her eyelids drifted shut. Just giving her pleasure made him harder.

"Yes." Heather threw her head back, a moan of gratification escaping her mouth as he flicked her nipple with his tongue.

"What about this?" His teeth nipped at her as he gently stroked her other nipple with his fingers.

"Oh, yes." It had been so long—too long, she realized, since she had last been intimate with him. "Mmm." She bit her lip as she tried to control the surge of need ripping through her as he took her into his mouth.

Heather pushed her hips closer, beginning a rhythmic movement against his burgeoning sex. He arched up in response, groaning with pleasure as he turned his attention to her other breast.

"Honey, slow down." She'd stolen his control. He grunted, clenching his teeth, fighting against the tide of demanding need rushing through him, wanting to prolong the escalation of desire, to savor every moment with her. His hands tugged the bottom of her swimsuit down. As she wriggled out of it, Justin ran his finger between her thighs. He sucked in a hard breath when her hands started to fumble with the waistband of his trunks; then he lifted his hips, helping to free himself. Then she touched him and he came apart inside.

Heather slid her hand around him, as he slipped his

finger inside her. Her mouth crashed against his while her hips rocked back and forth. She began moving more quickly, and he knew she was about to crest, enjoying the gratification her body demanded. "Wait," he pleaded, needing to be inside her.

He lifted her and set her over him, then groaned deep in his throat as she enveloped his sex. It had been so long since he'd been with her. He hissed as her body adjusted to his. She was tight, so tight that the realization that she hadn't been with anyone else hit him, and his heart slammed against his rib cage. Her hips undulated, driving back and forth, meeting the force of his as he moved inside her.

"Justin." She cried out her pleasure and her pupils dilated.

Knowing she was near climax, he pumped harder and faster, giving her the full use of his body, gritting his teeth, holding back his own pleasure until he was sure she was riding the peak of her own.

Then he fell over the edge into oblivion, calling her name as he rode the erotic waves with her.

Justin woke up alone the next morning.

He sat up stiffly and rubbed his hands through his hair, then listened to see if he could hear Heather. Her absence from his bed told him he might have had the pleasure of her body the night before, but that her trust wasn't as easily earned. Disappointment and annoyance rippled through him. When he didn't hear any sign that she was even in the hotel suite, he got out of bed, pulled on the jeans she'd convinced him to buy, and went to find her.

She was sitting on the small sofa with her back to him. As he approached her, Justin wondered if he was imagining her shoulders tensing. He walked up behind her and slid his hands over them. "Good morning," he whispered, then leaned down and nuzzled her neck.

"Morning."

She shifted slightly, stiffening when his lips caressed the sensitive area behind her ear. Justin frowned.

What the hell had happened between last night and this morning?

Circling the sofa, Justin stopped in front of her. She looked up, gave him a brief, unfocused glance, then went back to reading the newspaper in her hands. Frustrated, he shoved his hands in his pockets and stared at her.

"All right, let's talk about it."

Practically ignoring him, Heather continued to read without looking his way. "What?"

"Well, for starters, the disappearing act you pulled this morning."

That got her attention, and she lifted her face. Her gaze didn't quite connect with his. "I don't know what you're talking about." Her tone was evasive.

"The hell you don't," Justin stated, showing his annoyance.

She didn't say a word, and his frustration increased, bordering on anger. "Why weren't you in bed with me this morning?" he demanded, knowing he was letting his irritation show, but at the moment not caring. "You're not usually an early riser, so since you're up and dressed, I have to believe you're avoiding me."

She nibbled at her lip. "I, uh, I didn't want you to get the wrong impression."

Justin clenched his jaw. "And exactly what impression are you worried about?" he demanded. "The impression that you *enjoyed* making love last night? Or that you weren't sorry then, but you *are* now?"

Heather charged to her feet. "No, that's not what I'm talking about." Fire ignited in her eyes.

Confusion whipped through him, and he pulled his hands from the pockets of his jeans to rub the back of his neck. He couldn't figure her out for the life of him. "What *are* you trying to say?" He'd thought they'd crossed a barrier between them. He was disconcerted, realizing that apparently she didn't feel the same way.

She turned away and walked to the window, stared out at the traffic on the street far below. "Last night doesn't change anything."

Justin felt a knot forming in his gut. "What?"

She turned and faced him squarely, determination in the lift of her jaw. "Don't get me wrong. I wanted it as much as you did." The blatant admission caused her cheeks to redden.

Justin had a feeling he knew where she was headed, but he decided to let her spell it out. "I'm glad to hear it." His irritation was dampened by her admission, but only minimally.

"I just don't want you to think that everything's fine and we're back to where we were before..." She let her words drop off.

He stalked over to her, his expression fierce. "You're dead wrong, Heather. Last night changes everything." Before she could react, he grabbed her arms and dragged her against him, then forced her face up so he could look into her eyes. "I was wrong before to let you go. It won't happen again."

Heather was prevented from answering when the phone rang, interrupting them. With obvious reluctance, Justin let her go to cross the room and snatch it up. As he talked, she ran her gaze over him, and her body responded to the sight of him barely dressed. His shoulder and arm muscles rippled as he set the receiver back in its cradle. As he turned to face her, Heather immediately knew something was wrong.

"What is it?"

Concern etched his handsome features. "That was Miranda. Ryan's been hospitalized."

He was obviously shaken, and Heather went to him. "Oh, my. Is it serious?" she asked.

"His heartbeat is irregular, and they don't know what's causing it."

The concern over their own problems was forgotten for the moment, and Heather went into his arms, offering him comfort. Though he hadn't been a part of the Fortune family long, she could see on his face the impact of the news. Ryan's illness was a threat to Justin's new family, and he wasn't ready to confront what it might mean.

While Justin was bathing, Heather quickly called her mother to check on Timmy. She'd barely had enough time to tell Kathryn how things were going before she heard him turn off the shower. Her heart hammered as she hurriedly hung up the telephone. The deceit was beginning to take its toll on her. She didn't know how much longer she could go on with her ruse.

Though she wanted more than ever to tell him about his son, she didn't feel they'd worked through any of the problems that had caused their breakup.

Making love hadn't changed anything—except that it had heightened her awareness of him.

She wanted to talk to him, to really know how he'd felt when they lost their child—but right now his family needed him. Or, she thought, *he* needed to be with *them.* Heather willingly pushed aside her feelings in deference to the Fortunes, who were undergoing a more immediate crisis.

Together they went to hospital to be with Miranda and the rest of the family. Dr. Maggie Taylor, a hematologist and toxicology expert, had been assigned to Ryan's case. Though she had no answers yet, she met with the Fortune's briefly to update them on Ryan's condition. Heather was once again impressed by her husband's genuine concern for his uncle and by the way this large family pulled together for one of their own.

She could see changes in Justin—in the way he treated her, and in the way he was beginning to accept the Fortunes into his life. The spark of hope in her heart grew even stronger. If they could open up their hearts to each other, as well, maybe their marriage could work. And maybe, just maybe, last night really was a start in that direction.

Later that evening after dinner, they sat on one of the benches along the River Walk, talking a little about her job as a teacher and what the past year had been like for them both.

Then Justin stunned her by saying, ''I wish things had been different.'' He looked away, his gaze focused on a young family nearby. The father was pushing a stroller with a toddler, and his young wife held the hand of a little girl of about four. ''I wonder sometimes what our lives would be like if we'd never lost the baby.''

Heather stared at the couple. "I do, too. I wanted the baby so much. It was a part of me, a part of us. When I lost it, I thought that it was my fault somehow, that I'd caused it.''

Justin reached over and took her hand, gently stroking it as he talked. "It wasn't your fault, Heather. The doctors told us that sometimes miscarriages just happen and that there was nothing you could have done to prevent it.''

Tears glistened in her eyes as she looked directly at him, and Justin's skin turned ashen. Never had he believed she would think he had blamed her. Anguish twisted his features. Because he'd been unable to talk to her, he'd made her believe she'd been responsible? "Believe me, honey, I never blamed you. Not for a minute," he whispered fiercely. "I just didn't know what to say to you to make you feel better. I wanted to comfort you, but I felt like you were pulling away from me. There wasn't anything I could do to stop it.''

"Oh, Justin.'' She grasped his hand, then both of his surrounded hers.

"I'm sorry. I wish I'd been able to talk to you. I just couldn't bring myself to.''

She was startled by his admission. "Why *did* you walk away?'' she asked, staring into his eyes. Hurt vibrating from deep inside made her chest ache. "I thought you loved me.''

"You know I did.''

"You never said it.''

He flinched, the accusation stinging. She was right, of course, and he couldn't deny it. To him, words were not important. He'd never had anyone in his life say anything that he could believe. So instead, he'd shown Heather in every way he could how much she meant to him. He'd taken care of her. He'd been faithful. Occasionally, he'd brought her flowers. And he'd always stayed by her side when she was sick. He had done everything he was capable of, to let her know how much she meant to him.

Saying the words, well, that had been hard for him. A knot formed in his throat. He couldn't lose her again, not because of his inability to talk to her. Drawing a ragged breath, he forced himself to explain.

"I didn't grow up with anyone telling me anything except that I was a lot of trouble, or that I was in the way, or that they were sending me back into the foster care system," he said, his tone harsh. "When I was small, I foolishly hoped someone would come along and adopt me, take me home and love me. It never happened." His heart felt as if it had been stabbed as he relived the raw memories of a young child denied the basic emotional fulfillment of life.

"I can't imagine how difficult it must have been," she whispered.

"I tried so hard. I did everything they asked me to do. I didn't leave my clothes laying around. I cleaned up after myself." He shook his head and gave a short laugh. "I learned that lesson the hard way. Once, I got punished for leaving my school books on the bed instead of under it."

"They punished you for that?" she asked, astonished that people could be so hurtful.

He looked anguished. "I was put in a closet for hours, then sent to bed without dinner." He stopped speaking and looked away from her. Then he said, "Believe me, I never left anything out of place again. I never even unpacked my clothes after that. Whenever I went to a new home, I just left them in the bag I brought them in."

Heather was stunned, unable to speak. That explained his abnormal behavior when she'd asked him to pick up something he'd left lying around. "Justin, I'm so sorry."

It was obvious she was hurting for him, and her gaze filled with sympathy as she listened. "I don't want you to feel sorry for me," he said, his tone becoming slightly harsh. "I want you to understand who I am, where I came from. Talking was never easy for me, and to be honest, I'm still not comfortable, but I'm trying."

She waited patiently for him to go on, and after a brief hesitation, he continued. "A lot has happened over the past few months, and I'm learning how important family is. When I met my mother and the rest of the Fortunes, I wanted what they have—love for each other and their families. All I could think about was you and how much I need you in my life."

"Oh, honey, I need you, too. So much." Her voice broke, and she swallowed hard to gain some control over her jagged emotions. "But back then, I felt rejected by you. Losing the baby was so hard, and when you shut me out—"

"I felt you withdrawing from me, and I was devastated. My world was falling apart. I'd learned to control everything around me, but I realized I was powerless to stop what was happening between us."

Heather sighed and looked away from his intense gaze. "I resented that control," she admitted quietly.

She glanced back at him. "Oh, not at first," she said quickly, when she saw his facial muscles tense. "I'd never had anyone care so much for me that when we were first married, I let you make all the decisions concerning us. For a while, it made me feel special and protected. But after a while, I started to resent it. It seemed like the more I tried to show my own strength, the more you fought it."

"And now?" he asked, quietly studying her.

She hesitated, looking deep into his eyes, wanting him to understand that she'd changed. "I don't need you to take care of me anymore, Justin. It's important for you to realize that over the past year, I've grown a lot, learned that I'm stronger than I thought."

"And I was holding you back from learning that."

She nodded slightly, afraid to look at him, afraid not to. "When you asked me to come here, I was worried that perhaps we couldn't work things out between us because of your need to control everything and everyone around you." Her eyes watered. "But I see how you're trying to change. The Justin I knew before never would have behaved that way—he wouldn't have asked, he would have demanded it."

"Don't think I didn't want to," he said a bit reluctantly. "I'm making progress, but old habits die hard, honey." After pausing a moment, he went on. "Losing you showed me I could continue to control my feelings, but it would cost me in the end." He shook his head. "At the time, I told myself that you just needed some space, that things between us would get better. I was crushed when you asked for a separation."

She sighed heavily. "I never wanted you to leave. I think now that I was trying to shock you. I guess I was thinking you'd have to talk to me, somehow understand what I was feeling, help me through my own pain. I was just as wrong. I didn't talk to you, tell you what I was going through. I guess I *expected* you to know.'' Her eyes welled with tears; the droplets dripped from the corners and rolled down her cheeks. ''When I was a teenager and my father left, I felt so rejected by him.'' Her shoulders slumped. ''I guess I never let it go. When you agreed to the separation, I saw it as you rejecting me, too.''

He touched her face, then dashed tears from her cheeks with the pads of his thumbs. ''Please don't cry.'' Realizing where they were and not wanting to cause a scene, he said, ''Come on, sweetheart, let's go.'' Standing, he gently tugged her from her seat on the bench. Hand in hand, they walked back to the suite.

As they stepped inside, Justin slipped his arms beneath her legs and carried her to the bedroom. Once there, he laid her on the bed, then stretched out beside her and gathered her against him.

Sighing, he kissed her brow. ''Heather, I'm so sorry. I wish I'd handled things differently. I'm going to try really hard to be more open with you about what I'm feeling.''

''We both made a lot of mistakes,'' she said, smoothing the hair from his forehead.

He touched his lips to hers, slipping his tongue out and running it over them. Her arms twined around his neck, and she held his mouth to hers, deepening the kiss, until they had to break apart to breathe.

Justin started fumbling with her shirt, yanking it out of her pants. ''I love you, Heather.'' He kissed her mouth again, then gazed into her beautiful green eyes, eyes shining now with deep feeling and love. "I always have."

Heather smiled at him and he grinned lasciviously. "Let's make a baby," he whispered fiercely.

Ten

Heather touched his lips with her finger, stopping him from speaking, her heart beating hard and fast against her ribs. "Make love to me, Justin. Love me like you used to."

"Try and stop me," he whispered, his voice thick with need. He had unbuttoned all the buttons of her blouse and was busy working it off her shoulders. She slipped her arms free, which left her clad only in her bra and pants.

"You're overdressed," she complained, smiling seductively.

"Let's do something about that." He lifted himself up, as she tugged his shirttail out. Moments later, he unfastened her bra and tossed it away. Then, finally, they were skin to skin. Sealing her mouth with his, Justin kissed her long and hard.

Heather moaned deep in her throat, as he cupped

her breast. She ran her palms over the corded muscles of his back, gently raking his skin with her nails. His mouth left hers, only to return again and again. Then he was pressing hot, wet kisses to her neck. Then lower. When his tongue touched one hardened nipple, she arched her back, offering him more of herself. He gently teased first one peak, then the other.

When he stroked her belly with his tongue, she writhed beneath him, her hands in his hair, guiding his path. His hand found the button on the front of her slacks, and she stopped his progress by grabbing at it with her hands. "No, wait. The lights," she whispered.

Justin grinned wickedly and gazed into her eyes. "Leave them on. I want to look at you." He started to reach for the snap of her pants, but stopped when she spoke again.

"No, please turn them off," she whispered.

Again Justin hesitated, his expression questioning her reserve. "We've made love many times during the day, sweetheart. You never used to be shy." He touched her breast with his tongue, and she moved her hips in response.

"Please, Justin. Just for now."

Shrugging, he humored her and reached over to switch off the light. Moonlight shining through the sheer curtains cast the room in shadows. Justin shed the rest of his clothes as quickly as Heather had, then he returned to her.

Beginning at her belly, he lowered his mouth and touched her navel, then ran his tongue lower. Then lower still to the soft petals of her womanhood. Heather arched her back, and she spread open for him.

She cried out with pleasure as he stroked her, and he nearly lost his control.

"Please, Justin. Take me. Take me now," she pleaded, mindless, lost in the erotic ecstasy of his caresses.

Justin moved quickly, spreading her legs wide with his thigh. Then he sheathed himself inside her sweet warmth, gritting his teeth, holding back his own pleasure. She reached for him, and he covered her with his body, finding her mouth and kissing her deeply. Her hips rocked as he surged into her over and over again. "Heather." Her name came out hard, and he grunted as he felt her reach the peak of her desire.

Justin's control snapped. He tightened his arms around her, molding her to him as he climaxed.

Moments later, he shifted his weight from her and snuggled next to her. He rested his cheek on her breast, and she sighed with pleasure.

Let's make a baby.

His words reverberated through her mind, mocking her, and she considered telling him about Timmy right then. He would be so happy to learn of his son.

She started to speak, then hesitated, and fear prevented her from saying the words. Weighing her options, she thought it wiser to wait until morning. It was only a few hours longer.

But there were flaws in her reasoning, and she wrestled with her conscience for a few minutes. The best thing was to tell him right now, while they were still in each other's arms, sated from sharing their emotions, their innermost feelings and the intimacy of their bodies.

She made her decision. "Justin?" she whispered softly. She trailed a finger lovingly down his spine.

"Justin?" But he didn't stir. Heather could hear his even breathing, and she realized he'd fallen asleep.

He'd know in a few hours, she assured herself. Her heart swelled with joy. She so much wanted to share the news of his son with him! But she could wait until morning. They had forever now.

Justin slowly opened his eyes and, blinking a few times, made the adjustment to daylight. He stared with heartfelt wonder at his beautiful wife. Lying on her back and still lost in sleep, her arms rested above her head. The sheet covered most of her body, stopping just above the rosy nipples of her breasts. He was already used to having Heather in his bed again, and he couldn't imagine a time when he wouldn't want her there. She was his life, his reason for living. His heart swelled with love for her.

He'd reached for her during the night and she'd come into his arms willingly, half asleep but easily aroused. They'd loved each other until they were both exhausted and had then drifted off into a dream-filled state. Just looking at her now ignited a fire in his groin.

Moving closer to her, Justin slowly tugged the sheet down, baring her to him. He softly touched the tip of her breast, watching it pucker in response even as she slept. She moaned quietly when he trailed his finger down her middle. Her head turned toward him when he pressed a kiss to her stomach. He rested his head there, and ran his palm gently over her smooth, delicate skin. She was so lovely. And she was his.

He raised himself over her and touched his tongue to her, then kissed the sensitive area between her legs, initiating a response from her body that even sleep couldn't prevent.

He couldn't get enough of her.

Then he saw them.

Two tiny white marks, each about an inch long, embedded in the delicate skin near her hip. Puzzled, he ran his gaze from the tuft of soft curly hair between her legs to her breasts, then down along her left side.

Two more—and another not far away near the top of her thigh.

Frowning, he ran his finger over one.

Stretch marks. What the hell? His brows furrowed as he thought about them. Heather had never been big, so they definitely hadn't come from losing weight, he reasoned. Then where? Her pregnancy had ended in the first trimester, so he ruled that out as a cause.

"Heather," he whispered softly. He moved up a little so he could see her face. "Heather."

"Mmm, what?" she murmured, still in a light sleep. She frowned.

"Wake up, honey." He kissed her lips, and her eyelids fluttered open. She gazed up at him and a slow, sexy smile formed on her lips. Justin felt his heart lurch.

He grinned, his eyes crinkling at the corners. "Not that I'm complaining, because I think your body's beautiful," he began, "but how'd you get these?"

Heather felt his thumb rub gently over an area near her hip. The hazy look in her eyes cleared as they opened wider. "What?"

"These marks," Justin said again, curiosity in his voice as he glanced at them again. "They look like stretch marks."

She didn't say a word. Just stared at him. But Justin saw the warm flush rise in her cheeks as guilt crept over her features.

He sat up and stared down at her, pondering her response. "They are stretch marks, aren't they?"

Realizing she was caught in the web of her own deceit, Heather nodded without speaking.

"Where did they come from?"

She looked away and stiffened. Her behavior had a strange effect on him, frightening him. Justin had a sick feeling in his belly as he watched her edge herself into a sitting position and draw the sheet over her naked body.

"Justin, first, you have to believe I was going to tell you."

"Tell me what?" He still wasn't sure what was happening. He just knew it wasn't good by the way she was looking at him, her eyes filled with panic.

She covered her mouth with her hands, and tears sprang to her eyes. She shook her head. "Please don't hate me." Gasping for air, she started rocking back and forth, staring at the bedspread.

Don't hate me? Dumbfounded, Justin started to reach for her, but she recoiled from his touch. His entire body froze. "Calm down, honey. What is it?" He sucked in a hard breath and braced himself, as she lifted her tear-filled gaze to his.

"You have a son. His name is Timmy."

Justin went still. "What?"

"I know I should have said something before now," Heather blurted, "but I wanted to give us a chance together. I wanted the same thing you did, to make our marriage work. I—"

He flew off the bed and stood beside it, staring

down at her. "Wait. What are you talking about?" His tone had changed, becoming nearly lethal as his mind began to comprehend her words.

"I was pregnant when you left me."

Shock and disbelief quickly gave way to anger as he snatched his clothes from the floor. "Pregnant." As he jerked on his pants, he repeated the word as if he didn't understand the meaning. The disgust in his eyes told her he understood all too well.

"Yes. I was going to tell you," she said quickly, "you know, in the beginning. But you never even called me the entire year we were apart. I thought if you didn't care about me, you wouldn't care about our child," she explained, trying to make him understand her actions. "I hardly knew you those last few months. We barely spoke."

Justin glared down at her, anger sweeping through him and charging the atmosphere of the room. "That didn't stop you from having sex with me the last weekend we were together," he reminded her, his tone accusing.

"I was trying to save our marriage!"

Justin stalked away, then swung around and pinned her with a brutal look. "By lying to me?" he demanded hotly. "By keeping my son from me?" His clenched his fists, stunned at her deception. "I'll admit I'm not an expert on love, but I don't think that's how it works, sweetheart." The endearment dripped with sarcasm.

"I was hurting and alone." She tried again to make him understand.

"Well, guess what, sweetheart? You don't own the title on pain." He pointed a finger at her. "It hurt me to lose that baby, too. Did you even realize that? Or did you think I was so empty-hearted that I wouldn't care?'' Bone-crushing pain crashed down on him. That she believed him incapable of these emotions hurt more than her lies. That she believed he wouldn't want to know about his son...

Heather stared at him, horror on her face.

''Where is he?'' Justin demanded.

''He...my mother has him. He's staying with her at our house.''

Our house. The words rolled off her tongue so easily, it made him sick.

Justin staggered, then righted himself by bracing his hand against the wall. ''Why, Heather? Why didn't you tell me before?'' he demanded. ''I was there in the house with you—'' He stopped speaking, remembering her reluctance to let him in their house. ''Where was he? Where was my son when I was there?'' His voice rose a notch, bordering on shouting. He didn't care. He wanted answers.

''When you first came to the house, he was at Mom's.''

''I don't understand how you could do this to me.'' Despair racked his body. Everything she'd said had been a lie. He stared at her as she clutched the sheet, covering herself. Everything they'd *done* had been a lie.

''Justin—''

''No!'' he said harshly, rounding on her. ''I don't want to hear any more of your lies. All of this—'' he swept the room with his hand ''—was supposed to be for us. I was trying to reestablish the trust between us and all the while, you were deceiving me.''

Heather was still shaking, but she got out of the bed, wrapping the sheet around her body. ''Everything was happening so fast. You walked back into my life, then wanted to whisk me off to Texas. I started to tell you about the baby, but I knew you'd be angry."

"You're damn right, I'm angry!"

"I know. I know. And you have every right to be, but believe me, after last night, what we shared, well, I was going to tell you this morning."

"How convenient for you to admit that now."

"I was!"

"Yeah? Well, I was stupid enough to believe you once. I won't make the same mistake again." Justin suddenly remembered her quick excuse when he'd picked up the pacifier at the school that day. And only last night, she'd asked him to lower the lights...so he wouldn't see her scars.

She's been lying to me all along, said a voice in his head. *She went to extremes to keep my son from me.* His heart ached with the knowledge that she'd had plenty of opportunities to tell him, and yet she'd chosen not to.

She had a year to tell me.

"It's true!" she insisted. Heather had expected him to be angry, but she'd believed he'd be reasonable when she explained her feelings.

He turned away and grabbed his suitcase from beside the bed.

"What are you doing?"

For a moment he didn't answer. Then, with very deliberate movements, he faced her again, his expression devoid of every emotion except contempt. "I'm going to get my son. I suggest you get dressed if you want to go with me."

* * *

Justin held on to his anger as a shield against his feelings for Heather. He'd won her back, only to lose her again. He couldn't trust her now, not after the lies she'd told him. He'd never believed her capable of repeatedly lying to him. They'd conceived a child together, and she'd never told him. His jaw worked back and forth as he mulled over the past few hours.

You promised you'd never let her go again.

This was different, he justified to himself. *She* was the one who'd lied to him. This was *her* doing. Heather wanted him to believe part of this fiasco was his fault, but he wasn't culpable, and he wasn't going to let her put the blame on him. That would be playing right into her hands. Annoyance and humiliation warred within him. He'd thought he was so smart, charging back into her life and claiming her as his own.

It was discouraging to realize that he couldn't control his own destiny. Every time he thought he was making progress, life kicked him in the teeth. He'd let down his guard last night, and had let her get too close to him. Now he was paying the price.

She moved in her seat and her leg brushed his. A bolt of awareness shot through him, and he cursed beneath his breath. Memories of their lovemaking assailed him, and right on the tail of that memory came the sound of her voice, confessing her lies.

You have a son. His name is Timmy.

He wouldn't give her the power to hurt him again. He'd taken worse from the foster families he'd lived with, but he'd never believed Heather was capable of causing him this kind of pain.

* * *

Heather was out of the car before Justin had a chance to kill the engine. She rushed up the steps to her house, anxious to see her baby. She'd called her mother before leaving San Antonio to let her know they'd be arriving. Kathryn had been full of questions, but Heather had only had time to tell her the barest facts, before Justin had walked into the room.

She unlocked the door now and swung it open so hard that it slammed against the wall. "Mom?" Hearing sounds coming from the kitchen, she rushed in that direction. "Mom!"

Kathryn walked through the kitchen door and into the foyer with Timmy in her arms, almost running into her daughter. "Hi, honey," she said, her greeting warm and sincere. "Timmy, look who's here!" She slipped her grandson to her daughter as she embraced her.

Heather half cried and half laughed as she hugged her baby to her. "I've missed you so much!" Timmy gave her a bright smile, and she kissed his little cheeks. Then she turned toward Justin, and her own smile faded as she faced his embittered expression. She felt a stab of pain. Heather glanced at her mother, whose troubled look signaled her awareness of the tension. Prudently, she kept silent.

Heather looked back at Justin, and took a deep, stabilizing breath. "This is Timmy, your son," she told him, her voice softening as she hugged her baby close. "Timmy, this is your daddy."

Justin reached out his arms, and Heather gave him the baby. Having no experience with children, he wasn't sure what to do, but instinct took over. He cradled his son to his chest, slipping a hand behind his back to guard against his wriggling out of his arms.

Justin's heart melted a little, easing his anguish a fraction. The little boy had brown hair and the famous Fortune blue eyes.

Your son.

Unable to talk, Justin just stared at the baby in wonder. It was Kathryn who suggested they sit in the den and get comfortable. She watched her son-in-law holding his baby and gave her daughter a reassuring hug.

While Justin held Timmy, Heather asked, "How did everything go?"

"Like clockwork," Kathryn assured her. "How did you like San Antonio?"

"It was lovely." She started to comment further, but Timmy began to fuss. Heather went to him, and when she held out her arms, Justin passed him back without objecting.

"He's been a little fussy this afternoon. I'm not sure why. I was just getting ready to feed him, when you came in," Kathryn said. "Let me get his bottle."

"No, I'll get it," Heather insisted, diverting her gaze from Justin. She was already walking away before Kathryn could object.

Silence fell, shrouding the atmosphere.

Justin rubbed his jaw as he met Kathryn's direct gaze. "Kathryn, it's good to see you," he offered, not positive of the reception he'd get. He felt sure Heather had briefed her mother on why they'd returned so suddenly.

Kathryn eyed him speculatively. "It's been a long time, hasn't it."

Justin nodded, knowing there was something more than casual conversation on her mind.

Her expression softened. "She *was* going to tell you, you know. We talked about it often."

Justin made a disgruntled sound. "And what was your position?"

"I encouraged her to call you."

"As you said, it's been a long time. A whole year. She sure took her time about it," he stated, his tone cutting.

Kathryn looked him right in the eye. "And exactly what would you have done if she'd called you when she'd first learned she was pregnant?"

"You damn well know what I would have done, Kathryn. I'd have come back."

She shook her head. "Exactly."

Justin frowned at her, annoyed that she seemed to be way ahead of him in the conversation. "Your point being?"

"She didn't want you to feel trapped into coming back to her. Heather has pride too, Justin."

Too. As in *just like you.* Justin held his tongue, as Heather came back into the room.

"Well, I guess since I'm not needed around here, I'll take off."

"Mom, you don't have to go." Heather's voice held a plea that her mother wisely ignored.

"Oh, yes, honey, I do." She got up, and Justin stood at the same time. "I'll just get my things from the bedroom."

"Let me help you." Justin followed her out, then, when they returned, carried Kathryn's bags out to her car while she said goodbye to Heather. A minute later, as he was closing the trunk, Kathryn came out. She started to get in, then stopped and met Justin's gaze.

"Heather called me from Texas several times a day

to check on the baby,'' she volunteered. ''I got the impression things were going really well between you two.'' She waited, and when Justin didn't answer, she continued, ''Not once in the six years you and Heather were married did I ever butt into your business. But I'm going to make an exception this one time.'' She reached over the door frame of the car and squeezed his arm. ''You think good and hard about what's inside that house that you stand to lose.''

When he said nothing, she got in the car and drove away.

Eleven

Justin walked over to his car and pulled their luggage from the trunk. One thing he'd always admired about Kathryn was that she *did* mind her own business. Until now. As much as he'd wanted to argue with her, he hadn't even tried because he wouldn't have known what to say.

He'd missed his son growing in her womb, missed his birth. He would have liked to have been there for that—to see his son as he was brought into the world, to share that special moment with his wife. A new surge of anger swept through him as he stalked toward the house. As he walked inside, he set their suitcases in the foyer. Heather came in from the den.

"What are you doing?" she asked, when she saw his suitcases along with hers.

"Moving in. What does it look like?"

For a fraction of a minute, she foolishly believed

he'd softened, that he was willing to forgive her. Then her gaze went to his face, and his stern expression told her differently. Irritated, she said, "You can't move in here!"

"I assure you I can, and I am." He reached over and relieved her of Timmy, then tucked the baby in his arms. The child turned his gaze on the stranger holding him, and in that moment, Justin lost his heart.

"You can't just move in here," she repeated, her thoughts in turmoil. *Not after today. Not if you don't love me.*

Justin's lips flattened. "My name's still on the deed, isn't it?"

She opened her mouth to argue, then clamped it shut. Steam fairly rose from her.

He ignored the pull on his heart as he watched her fume. He didn't *want* to want her, hated that he couldn't control his need for her. He turned away, and blocked her from his sight. "I want to be near Timmy. I want him to know who I am." His son was never going to wonder where he came from, or if he was loved.

He wasn't going to grow up without a father. Not the way Justin had.

Still holding the baby, Justin picked up his own suitcase and headed for the back of the house. He walked into the spare bedroom and deposited the suitcase on the floor with a loud *thud.*

It had taken every bit of his control not to turn in the opposite direction and head toward the bedroom he'd shared with Heather. Now that he'd had her back in his bed, it wasn't so easy to forget the softness of her skin, the taste of her body as he made love to her, the ease with which she welcomed him into her. Despite the stretch of time without her, she'd imbedded herself in his soul.

Damn her! She'd ruined everything!

Heather had been holding her breath, a little ray of hope inside whispering that he was going to insist that they sleep together. She realized it wasn't going to happen when he didn't even spare their bedroom a glance, and she felt foolish for letting her imagination run wild.

Hurt made her shoulders sag as she walked behind him. He'd fooled her, after all. Because he'd started to open up to her, she'd begun to think he had changed. But he hadn't, not really. She could easily see that he was falling back into his old pattern of closing himself off from her.

His rejection before had been difficult, but she'd managed to pick up her life and move on. But now— now Heather had had a glimpse of the happiness they could have shared.

As she watched him sit on the bed and talk to Timmy, an emptiness stole over her, robbing her of the ability to fight for him, for their marriage. If this was the way he wanted it, so be it. She wasn't going to risk her heart again.

They barely spoke to each other the rest of the evening, other than to talk briefly about what to eat for dinner. Their conversation was even stilted when Justin insisted on helping her with Timmy's bath. While Heather was disillusioned in him as her lover and partner for life, she couldn't have been more mistaken about his wanting to father his child. Every single moment the baby had been awake, Justin had been either holding him, feeding him or playing with him. When she put her son down for the night, she had to force Justin to leave the room, knowing Timmy wouldn't fall asleep unless left alone. Unaware of the strained relationship between his parents, the baby cooed in his crib, making them linger near him. Already, her child was learning how to manipulate them.

In the middle of the night, Heather came awake, startled out of a restless sleep. She sat upright in bed. The events of the previous day came rushing back at her as she threw back the covers, unsure of what had disturbed her sleep. An eerie feeling crawled slowly up her spine, and she slipped out of bed, pulling her robe on as she walked toward Timmy's room.

She stopped at the door, startled to find Justin already there, lifting their son in his arms.

"What is it? What's wrong with him?" she asked, looking at Justin in the little bit of light his night-light provided. Her anxious expression found his.

"I don't know." Sounding mystified, Justin patted Timmy's back, trying to quiet his whimpering. Heather reached for the baby. As Justin passed Timmy to her, the baby promptly threw up on them both. Most of it hit Justin in the chest, then slid down to the waistband of his pants.

"Oh, goodness."

Heather grabbed for a nearby cloth, and began cleaning Timmy. Justin tried his best to help, using another cloth to wipe himself and Heather. He felt more in the way than anything. Before he knew it, she had the situation under control. She redressed Timmy, then carried him with her as she went to her own room so she could change.

Justin met her in the hallway as he came out of the spare bedroom. His skin was pale, his expression concerned. "Is he all right? Isn't there a doctor you can call? Maybe we should go to the hospital.'' He felt helpless, and it disconcerted him.

Heather shook her head. ''Calm down. He doesn't feel feverish, so let's give it a little while. Maybe his dinner just didn't agree with him.'' She walked down the hallway toward the living room, Justin right on her heels, firing questions at her left and right.

''Is that possible?''

''Of course.''

''Why?''

She shrugged impatiently. ''I don't *know* why. He has a tiny tummy. Maybe he ate too much.''

''What are you going to do?'' he asked, as she sat down on the sofa. He couldn't believe she wasn't more concerned.

Heather gave him a barely patient look. ''Keep an eye on him. If he isn't better by morning, we'll take him to the doctor.''

Minutes turned into hours, hours into morning. Timmy was awake and fussy the entire time. Justin watched Heather tend to his son and tried to help her when he could. Mothering came easily to her, he decided, as she bathed the baby with a cool compress, fed him a little water in a bottle and patted his back.

Justin had never been around children enough to know what to do when one was sick. He was both amazed and impressed with his wife's ability to handle the situation. He took turns with her, walking Timmy when her arms tired.

As the sun was finally making its appearance, the baby began to tire, and Heather decided to take him to her bed and lie down with him. Though she didn't invite Justin into her bedroom, he followed her inside and sat in a nearby chair, as she settled the infant beside her.

A few minutes later they were both asleep. Tenderness filled Justin's heart, and he found it harder to hold on to his anger. He still didn't believe that Heather's actions were justified, but he had to ask himself if Kathryn was right. Were Heather and Timmy worth losing, just so he could hang on to his pride? To his anger?

She lied to you. Would she really have told you about your son if you hadn't gone to see her?

Despite his need to forgive Heather, his distrust was strong and deep. She was the only person in the world he had believed would never hurt him like this. He couldn't find the courage to trust her again.

By late that same evening, Timmy was his old self again, and Justin's anxiety eased. He spent the next two weeks just enjoying being a father. Maybe it was his imagination, but he was sure the baby recognized him now. Timmy cooed and smiled, when Justin blew lightly into his face. Justin wasn't sure, but it seemed to him that the baby even turned his head when he heard his dad's voice.

He was learning this father thing, and was amazed at what time and attention a little tyke could demand. They were either feeding him, cleaning him or entertaining him most of the day. There were a couple of breaks when Timmy took naps, but even then, Justin felt on edge, just waiting for his son to awaken so he could hold him.

And his heart ached just as hard as he watched his wife. She was everything a man could want—a beautiful woman, a wonderful mother. Justin worked hard on his emotions, trying to put what she'd done in perspective, trying to understand her motives.

He wanted them to be a family, wanted to be a part of his son's life. If he could come to terms with her deceit, they could start all over, be a family. But as hard as he tried, he couldn't get past the pain. Even knowing he was risking what he most wanted in his life, he couldn't find it in his heart to forgive her.

Heather was just as aware of relations between them worsening. She walked into the den and saw Justin playing with Timmy, giving the gurgling baby all his attention. An empty ache settled inside her as she watched him entertaining his son. She couldn't go on like this, she decided. She thought she'd go crazy if she didn't get a break from the tension.

The telephone rang, and Heather picked it up, then, after a few moments, handed Justin the receiver.

"It's your mother," she said, her expression questioning.

Justin covered the mouthpiece. "I gave her this number. I wanted her to know where to reach me." Leaving Heather with Timmy, he walked out of the room, stopping just outside the door.

Heather's first thought as she listened to him talking was that for someone who a few short months ago hadn't known who his family was, he was certainly in close contact with them. Then she overheard Justin promising to return to Texas, and felt a sense of relief. Since they weren't getting along that well, she could deal with a few days alone with her son. But when she heard Justin telling Miranda that he'd bring Timmy with him, she saw red.

As soon as he disconnected the call and came back into the room, she jumped on him. "Did you just tell your mother that you're taking Timmy with you?" she demanded, picking the baby up from the floor and standing in front of her husband, her expression challenging, her eyes blazing.

"Yes," he said, his tone curt. "Thanks to you, she has a grandson she's never seen. I promised I'd bring him with me."

Heather's face contorted with fury. Here again, he was making decisions that affected her, and now Timmy, without even consulting her. "You should have asked me first."

"You should have told me I have a son," Justin countered. She flushed, and he let his gaze sweep her, wishing again that he could let this ache in his heart heal. But how could he ever trust her again?

Heather ignored the barb. "What did Miranda want?"

"I need to sign some papers." Justin had been expecting the call. "Miranda and her sister-in-law, Mary Ellen, are having some legal documents prepared, declaring that I'm Miranda's son and that as such, I'm entitled to part of the Fortunes' wealth."

The fact that he would be receiving ten-million dollars was not nearly as surprising as learning that he had a three-month-old child. He didn't need the money. What he really needed was peace in his heart. He just couldn't seem to find it.

"And I *am* taking my son to Texas to meet his grandmother. You're welcome to accompany us," he said stiffly. The offer didn't sound sincere.

"Well, thank you so much," Heather returned, looking as if she could murder him. "And don't you even think I *won't* be going wherever my son is going."

* * *

Traveling with a child had taken a lot more planning and packing than Heather had anticipated. By the time they arrived at the hotel in San Antonio, Justin had arranged for a crib to be delivered. Timmy was exhausted, so Heather put him right to bed.

That left her and Justin alone. Ignoring him, she sat on the edge of the bed and watched her son in slumber, exhausted from his travels. He was the innocent pawn in this war of hearts. It didn't seem fair. It needed to end, and she faced the fact that Justin was right. A baby couldn't heal their marriage.

She had thought that Timmy would bring them closer together. Instead, Justin was using Timmy, and the fact that she'd kept the baby a secret, to keep her at a distance. She knew she was at fault. She should have told Justin about Timmy when she'd first gotten pregnant.

Had she deliberately convinced herself that keeping Timmy's birth a secret was the best thing, so she wouldn't have to see Justin again? So she wouldn't have to face her own fears?

All men aren't like your father. Her mother's words came back to haunt her, reminding her that she was still not giving her trust to Justin. If she'd trusted him from the beginning, none of this would have happened. He wouldn't have left her.

It was easy to give up, not to fight for him. Walking away was the coward's way.

Maybe Justin just wasn't ready to believe that she would have told him about their son. Maybe he just wasn't ready to let her back into his heart. Maybe he just needed some more time.

He'd been hurt so much throughout his life. He was

learning, too. Learning to love, to trust unconditionally. Heather told herself to be patient. Justin did love her. He couldn't make love to her so tenderly with love and passion if he didn't care for her. Those were the little hints that he'd given her to show her how much he cared.

Heather wasn't a quitter. She loved Justin, dammit!

She wasn't going to give up on him, wasn't ready to give up on their marriage.

She glanced at the clock on the bedside table. They weren't due to go to Miranda's house until the next afternoon. How was she going to get through the hours with Justin until then?

Formulating a plan, she decided to kill him with kindness. Her presence didn't seem to matter to him; he buried himself in work unless their son was awake, and then he spent his time with the baby. Heather straightened the room and picked up Timmy's things, making her presence known so that Justin couldn't totally ignore her.

She even dropped Timmy's toy on the floor then, as she bent to pick it up, she brushed Justin's arm with her hand, touching him a little longer than necessary. He tensed and gave her a hard look, his eyes cold and distant. Her heart ached, but she continued moving about the room in his view, refusing to just disappear and cower from his black mood.

Justin tried his best, she'd give him that. During their meals, he ate in silence, until she began asking him questions about his mother and the meeting he was going to. He was evasive, short with his answers, but he did respond to her, and that was what was important.

She wondered what would happen that evening at

bedtime, since there was only the one bed. Maybe she could gain some ground there, she thought, planning a sneak attack on him as he slept beside her. Heather wasn't going to push too hard, because she wanted Justin to realize on his own that he loved her, that they had something special between them.

But as the evening passed, he made no mention of their sleeping arrangements.

When she decided to go to bed, Justin told her he had work to do and would be up late. Eventually she gave up and went to the bedroom alone. She stared at the bed they'd made love in, and tears gathered in her eyes.

How long was it going to take? she wondered. Feeling let down, she fell into bed, exhausted from her thoughts and troubles. Well, tomorrow was yet another day. She'd just start all over again with him.

She never heard Justin come into the room to bed, but the next morning she awoke and found him sleeping beside her. Unable to stop herself, she reached over and touched him, running her finger over his shoulder and arm. He stirred slightly, then settled back into sleep.

Heather moved closer to him, wanting to be next to him if only for a little while. She scooted until her body was close to him, then gently rolled over, letting her leg fall over his. Without waking him, she pressed even closer and snuggled up to him, resting her hand on his chest, thinking she would only lie there a few minutes. He would never have to know.

The next time she opened her eyes, Justin was staring at her with a dark, intense gaze. She thought she caught a look of tenderness in his blue eyes before he turned from her, got out of bed and went to take his shower.

That gave her hope. Maybe he was beginning to think about what he felt for her. Maybe he was beginning to realize what he stood to lose if he didn't let go of his anger. She'd give him some time to think about his feelings. After all, she hadn't known her own true feelings for some time. Not until Justin had come back into her life.

By the time she'd finished her shower, he was back at the desk working. Instead of wearing the casual jeans and shirts they'd bought together, he'd chosen one of his dark suits. Heather considered that another sign—a subtle one, but a sign just the same. He was distancing himself from her.

No longer able to endure his silence, a couple of hours before they were due to go to Miranda's, Heather confronted him. "I'd like to talk with you."

That got enough of his attention that he stopped what he was doing and looked at her, his eyes cold and unfeeling.

"You were right."

He raised a brow. Still he said nothing.

"About a child not being enough to save our marriage." She swallowed past the knot in her throat.

He sat back in his chair, but his shoulders tensed as if he was bracing himself for her words. "And?"

He wasn't giving her an inch. Heather fought for more. She believed the love he felt for her was still in his heart, but now it was buried beneath angry words and hurtful accusations—and her deceit.

Well, she couldn't pay forever. She motioned with her hands. "I...I don't want to live like this. Whatever it was we felt for each other—" She choked on the words and pressed a hand to her throat, willing herself to go on. "I know it's still there if you give us a chance."

"I don't know if I can trust you again." Without saying another word, he went back to his work.

"Can't we at least talk about it?" she demanded, hurt that he was pulling away, falling back into his old pattern of retreating from her. "Only days ago, you said you were trying to change, to learn to communicate."

Nothing. He didn't even look at her.

"Okay, Justin, I've told you how sorry I am. I was wrong to keep Timmy's birth a secret from you. But we were both wrong. If you ever believed that we could have a wonderful life together, then think about that now. I love you. I want this to work. I want us to be a family. Isn't that what you wanted, too?" When he didn't answer, she sighed with frustration and walked away, feeling as if she wasn't making any progress.

Was she a fool to keep trying?

Twelve

"**Oh**, my goodness. Would you look at this beautiful little one?" Miranda held out her arms, and Heather passed Timmy over.

"Justin, you and Heather have given me the greatest gift!" she exclaimed. "Another grandchild!" Despite her elegant appearance and demeanor, Miranda *ooh*ed and *ahh*ed all the way to the house.

"Come on in," she called, then led them to the living room. Miranda and Heather sat on the large couch, while Justin chose to sit across from them on a matching chair. "He's absolutely adorable."

Heather managed a smile, her heart aching. "Thank you. I'm sure Justin told you his name is Timmy."

Miranda nodded, glancing briefly at her daughter-in-law. Heather shifted her gaze to Justin, then back to his mother. His expression was stoic, his eyes cold.

Tension stretched between them. She managed to carry on a conversation with Miranda, while Justin sat across from them and said very little.

After a while, when Timmy began to get fussy, Heather mentioned that they'd have to be going soon. Miranda looked at Justin. "The meeting is set for four o'clock this afternoon. Is that convenient for you?"

"I don't see a problem with it. Will you and Timmy be all right while I'm gone?" he asked Heather as he stood and took Timmy's things from her so she could carry the baby.

She nodded. "Sure."

"I'll see you then," Justin told Miranda.

She walked them to the door, and Heather was sure that Miranda wasn't oblivious to the strain between her son and his wife. "Please bring Timmy back again soon."

A little while later, Heather changed Timmy's diaper, while Justin prepared his formula. Heather had taught him how, and he had a new respect for mothers in general—and his wife in particular, he admitted to himself.

Taking the baby from her, Justin settled himself on the sofa and touched the nipple of the bottle to his son's bow-shaped lips.

His son.

Justin's chest swelled with pride as he watched the bundle in his arms. Somehow, the tiny infant had captured his heart, easing the pain over the baby he and Heather had lost. A movement across the room caught his eye, and he lifted his gaze. Silently Heather moved about the room, tidying it up a bit, adding some organization to their surroundings.

Despite his feelings of betrayal, he watched her

graceful movements with fascination. In the space of a few months, he'd gone from living alone to acquiring a family.

Timmy's presence in his life made up for all the hardships he'd endured through the years—the abandonment; the torture of living with foster families who never wanted *him,* only the money he could bring them.

From the first moment he'd held his son, they'd bonded. He'd felt it in his soul. Everything Justin had ever wanted—a wife, a child, a home—was within his grasp.

Why couldn't he get past Heather's betrayal? Why couldn't he just let it go?

No answer came to him as he lifted his son in his arms and placed him on his shoulder.

His feelings for Heather were all mixed up inside him.

He loved her. He couldn't deny it. But he had to wonder if love was really enough to make them a family. Once again, he was in danger of losing everything he'd ever wanted.

"I'll be leaving soon. Should I put him in his crib?" Justin asked quietly so as not to awaken Timmy. Heather nodded, and he got up from the sofa and walked past her. After placing the baby in the crib, he turned back to her.

"Would you like some lunch?" he asked. "I can get you something from room service."

Heather's heart hammered. Well, that was a start. At least he didn't want her to starve to death. "No, thank you. I'm not hungry."

He put his hand in his pocket, and she could hear the jingle of his keys. "I guess I'll leave, then."

"Before you go—"

Her words stopped his movements, and he let go of the doorknob. "Yes?"

"I…want to talk to you."

"Go ahead."

She twisted her hands in front of her. "I've tried very hard to tell you how sorry I am, but you don't even want to talk about it. I thought we had at least learned something from our past mistakes."

"I thought I could trust you."

She visibly trembled under his cold stare. "I've asked you to forgive me. If you can't, if we can't talk about this, then maybe we should get a divorce," she said quietly.

His eyes narrowed on her. "A divorce?" he repeated.

She nodded. "Yes. I'm not saying it's what I want, but I'm not going to pay for my mistake forever."

He opened the door and turned to face her. For a moment, Heather thought he was going to say something further, but he just stared at her, then walked out, taking her heart with him.

Justin was met at the lawyer's office by his mother. Together they went inside the elite offices and were soon greeted by the attorney handling her holdings. The attorney showed them to an enormous conference room, and everything was ready for them. Along with the lawyer, she took a seat, but Justin remained standing.

The lawyer explained the details, then laid the pen on the papers. Miranda quickly put her signature on the correct lines. Then she turned the documents toward Justin. He hesitated, lifting his eyes to his mother. "You know I don't need this," he stated, uncomfortable with the whole idea of discussing money with her.

Miranda smiled at her very prideful son. "Yes, I know. You've done quite well for yourself. I don't know if it matters to you, but I'm proud of the man you turned out to be. Regardless of whether you need it, this money is your birthright. You're a Fortune, Justin, just like your sister and your cousins." She got up and walked around her chair to stand beside him. "Please."

He nodded and picked up the pen, then quickly and efficiently scrawled his signature on the lines indicated. Silence engulfed the room as the lawyer gathered the papers and excused himself.

"This makes you officially part of the Fortune family," she commented.

Family.

Being a part of a family was what he'd always wanted. Wasn't it?

Images of Heather and Timmy raced through his mind, and Justin shook his head, trying to clear his thoughts.

You and Heather and Timmy could be a family if you let go of the hurt and forgive her. Do you want to give them up?

Miranda's voice interrupted his thoughts. "Well, Emma's already signed hers. Storm and Jonas will be signing theirs soon. That leaves Holly Douglas."

"Holly?" Justin absently raised an eyebrow as he dropped the pen on the table.

"Yes. You remember I told you about Holly? We've been so fortunate with the rest of you that we

never expected she might not want to come here.''
Disappointment shadowed her expression.

"You can't force Holly to come here and be a part
of the Fortune family,'' he warned, gentling his tone,
not wanting Miranda to be disappointed.

"Yes, I know. But we can certainly try. We've
hired a bush pilot named Guy Blackwolf to find her
and bring her here. We're hoping she'll come
around.'' She smiled wryly and gently touched him
on the forearm. "You did, and so did Emma.'' Giving
him an affectionate pat on the arm, she said, "Justin,
I'm so happy to have you in my life.''

Miranda's fervent words touched a dark place in
Justin's heart. He opened his arms, and she went into
them. It was the first time he'd let anyone other than
Heather that close, and Justin closed his eyes as he
allowed himself to accept her affection. Then, without
thinking about it, he held her tighter, putting his past
behind him and accepting Miranda as his mother.

Accepting the Fortunes as his family.

He'd learned over the past few months that the Fortunes pulled together and truly cared about one another. They valued family relationships, above all,
loving each other despite any problems they faced.

Family. The world reverberated through his mind,
reminding him that because of his pride, he was going
to lose his little family. *If you let Heather go, you'll
be giving up your own dream. She and Timmy are
your family, too.*

He'd forgiven Miranda. In the deepest part of his
soul, he no longer held any resentment for her abandoning him and Emma. Didn't Heather, the woman
he loved, deserve the same forgiveness?

Justin could suddenly see that his own mistakes had

played a large part in his relationship with Heather, making him just as responsible for their marriage falling apart. If he'd been open and honest with her when she'd lost their baby, they never would have separated. He would have been there with Heather when she'd discovered she was pregnant again, would have been able to enjoy spoiling her during the ensuing months when she needed pampering.

She tried to tell you. You refused to listen.

He *was* guilty of not listening when she'd tried to explain to him. He'd been so hurt that he had closed his heart off from further pain. Being abandoned as an infant and growing up in foster care had made him feel unwanted and unloved. He'd never been with any one family long enough to learn how to trust another person. Every time he'd taken a chance and let down his guard, had started to accept the family he was with, he was taken away and shipped somewhere else.

So he'd protected his heart by not allowing another person close enough to hurt him. And he was going to pay the price by losing Heather if he didn't do something awfully damn quick to prevent it.

He stiffened and pulled away from Miranda.

"Justin?"

He looked at her absently, his thoughts on Heather.

"Justin, is there something wrong?" she asked. "I know it's none of my business—"

"Actually, yes."

"Darling, what is it?" Miranda asked with concern.

"I left something very important back at the hotel."

My heart.

Miranda stared at him with confusion.

Justin felt exuberant as the haze he'd been in totally lifted, clearing his thoughts. "Never mind. I need to go."

"Why?"

"Because I've got a marriage to save."

Justin couldn't get back to the hotel suite fast enough. He'd finally come to his senses, and he couldn't understand how he could have been so blind. He'd allowed his upbringing and his past insecurities to cloud his thinking, endangering his marriage and his relationship with his own son.

"Heather!" He rushed into the apartment, and the silence there hit him hard and fast. The hair on the back of his neck stood up when he realized that she and the baby weren't there. He felt as if he'd had the wind knocked out of him.

Glancing around the room, he noticed that the diaper bag was gone. He made a mad dash into the bedroom. Heather's things were still there. But the queasy feeling in his stomach intensified. She hadn't mentioned anything about going out.

Dammit, where was she?

She talked about a divorce. Maybe she left you.

No, she wouldn't do that.

Why not? Because you love her?

"God, yes," he said aloud, to no one but himself. "I love her." What a fool he'd been to hold onto his pain and anger. Dejectedly, he walked into the living area of the suite and sank into a chair.

What was he going to do? Where would she go? She hadn't taken her things, so maybe she hadn't gone far. Of course, she could have been so upset that she went without them.

His mind in turmoil, Justin stared blankly at the ceiling. He wanted to leave and search for her—but she could be anywhere. If she'd really left him, she'd be en route, so there was nothing he could do but sit and wait.

Hell, he *couldn't* just sit and do nothing. Getting out of the chair, he began to pace. He walked over to the window and looked out, hoping to see her, but knowing in his heart he wouldn't.

An hour passed, and Justin thought he would go crazy. Desperate, unable to stand doing absolutely nothing, he called Kathryn. She hadn't heard from her daughter. Cursing his stupidity and pride, he slammed down the phone. Then he heard the door to the suite open, and his gaze flew in that direction.

Heather stood in the doorway with Timmy in her arms.

Relief washed over him like a flood on dry, parched land. Thank God!

"Where have you been?" he demanded, then caught her defensive expression. "I'm sorry. I was worried." He swallowed hard.

"We went to the mall," she said, coming into the room and depositing Timmy in the crib. Putting some packages down, she turned to face her husband, saw the worry lines on his face. "Is everything all right?"

"I hope so."

Heather stared at him with open curiosity. Something was different about his manner, about the way he was looking at her. Like he was *relieved* to see her. Had he thought that she'd left him?

"A little while ago you talked about getting a divorce," he said, then shoved his hands in his pockets. "It made me stop and think about what I was doing to both of us.'' He glanced at his son, who lay sleeping, then turned his gaze back on Heather. ''To all of us.''

She didn't say anything, and he felt as if he was teetering on the edge of a cliff. ''I love you, Heather.'' He saw her shudder when his words registered, then she closed her eyes for a moment and took a deep breath.

She didn't believe him. The fear of losing her left a coppery taste in his mouth.

''I do love you,'' he said again, then moved toward her, stopping only inches away. She had to listen to him.

I promise I'll never let you go. His words came back to haunt him.

''I was a fool for not listening to you, for shutting you out again. God knows, I don't deserve it, but I'm asking you to give me another chance.''

Her gaze met his, and a rush of tears gathered in her eyes. ''I never meant to hurt you,'' she whispered, her voice cracking. ''I swear with all my heart that I didn't.''

Justin stared at her, so thankful that she was still standing there, that she hadn't left him. ''I think I know that now. I've made a lot of mistakes,'' he confessed. ''But the biggest one was not listening to you. I was so caught up in my own misery, I guess it was hard for me to see how much you were hurting, too.'' He stopped short of putting his hands on her shoulders. ''I was blinded by my pride and couldn't see what you were trying to tell me. You were right. We both made mistakes in the beginning. If I had shared what I was feeling when we lost the baby, none of this would have happened.''

"What are you saying?" She stared at him, her eyes still filled with caution.

"That I forgive you for not telling me about Timmy." He reached out and touched a lock of her auburn hair. "And I'm asking you to forgive me for leaving you."

Justin dropped his hand, unsure of what she was thinking.

Was he too late? he wondered.

"I love you, honey. I have since the day I married you. I couldn't say the words before, but I can now." His heart in his throat, he forged on, "I can't promise I won't make mistakes in the future, but I'll work on being more open about my feelings."

Overwhelmed with emotion, Heather sobbed, then rushed into his embrace. She knew at that moment just how much Justin had changed. "I didn't want to leave you," she murmured against his chest. "I love you so much." She trembled in his arms, and he gathered her closer. As she lifted her face to his, he kissed her hungrily, tasting the salt of her tears.

Heather couldn't believe she was being given this second chance for happiness. Sliding her arms around his neck, she molded her body to his. When he lifted his lips, she held his face with her hands and looked into his blue eyes. "I'm so sorry I didn't tell you about Timmy," she said, gasping for air as she continued to cry. "I was so afraid of being hurt again. I was only thinking of myself and not you."

"Hush, honey. I'm just as guilty. I didn't know how to be a loving, supportive husband. I thought if I provided well for you, that you'd love me."

"I did love you," she whispered fiercely. "I think after my father left me, I never trusted anyone but my mother. Then when I met you, I wanted to believe you would never hurt me, but I couldn't. So I shut a little of myself away. I had to protect myself from being hurt again. I never let you close enough to me, and I blamed you when you left.''

"I shouldn't have walked away from you.'' His jaw tightened, then relaxed. "Heather, you know how I was raised. I didn't let anyone close to me. Then I met you, and took a chance. When we lost the baby, I thought that if I gave you some space, you'd come around. I couldn't talk to you about it, and I know now that by being distant, I made you think I didn't care. But I did. I wanted you to need me. I thought by needing me, you'd love me.''

"Oh, Justin.'' She sighed, then hugged him to her. "I'm so sorry. For everything.''

"I know. I really do. So am I. I guess it took finding my birth mother to teach me about trust and love. When I met the Fortune family, I realized how much they cared about each other. Family was important to them, important enough for them to find me. I knew then that I wanted the same happiness, and that I had given it up when I left you. So I came back for you.'' He kissed her mouth, then frowned.

"When I walked up and saw you there with Dailey, I wanted to smash his face,'' he admitted, his voice grim.

"I thought you were going to.''

"I would have, if he hadn't taken his hands off you.'' Justin kissed her thoroughly. "You were mine. You always will be. I love you so much. Believe me, you're never going to get away from me again.'' He kissed her again and again, savoring her taste. His heart was beating so fast, he thought he was in danger of having an attack.

Heather stared up at him. "About your possessive-ness"

"I'll work on that, too," he promised.

Smiling, she answered, "Well, don't work too hard on it."

"Wench," he said, kissing her neck, then he gazed into her emerald-green eyes. "I'll love you for the rest of my life. That's a promise, sweetheart."

Heather lifted her mouth for his kiss. It was a promise she believed.

* * * * *

*Find out what happens
when Guy Blackwolf goes to Alaska
to meet lost heir Holly Douglas in*

FORTUNE'S SECRET DAUGHTER,

*coming only to Silhouette Desire
in September 2001.*

*And now, for a sneak preview,
please turn the page.*

One

The storm came on fast and hard, and slapped at the tiny seaplane as if it were a pesky gnat instead of three thousand pounds of metal. Thunder boomed and a second assault on the plane tipped the nose dangerously downward. Metal groaned while the pilot swore, struggling to hold on to the wheel and stay in control.

"Come on, sweetheart, stay with me," Guy Blackwolf hissed through clenched teeth. "We've seen worse than this."

Thick clouds swallowed machine and man whole. A jagged bolt of lightning exploded not more than twenty feet from the plane's left wing, momentarily turning Guy's world a brilliant, blinding white. He blinked furiously, tightened his grip on the throttle and eased the plane's nose level, while the wind rocked the wings like a teeter-totter.

"Steady, steady," he coaxed with the patience of a lover. "That's my girl."

He knew he was close. He could see the tops of the trees thirty feet below, and according to his instruments, Twin Pines Lake was two hundred feet ahead. Two more minutes and he'd be safe and sound, gliding smoothly over the water to shore.

He could do it. He *would* do it. He owed a friend a favor, and he refused to let anything—even a miserable storm in the wilderness of Alaska—get in his way. Mother Nature might be one tough broad, but Guy Blackwolf had yet to meet a female that he'd let get the better of him.

The storm opened up like the jaws of a giant beast and closed around the plane, then gave a savage shake. The throttle shook fiercely under Guy's hand, but he held firm, eyes narrowed, jaw tight. Just another hundred feet. Piece of cake, he told himself as he eased the plane down.

He gave a hoot of victory as he broke through the blanket of thick gray and the lake emerged below him. He spotted the dark-blue Land Rover parked close to the north bank, knew that the woman was waiting for him. Well, not for *him,* he thought with a smile. Holly Douglas thought he was merely bringing supplies. He'd let her keep thinking that, until he assessed the situation. She wasn't going to like it, but when the moment was right, he'd tell her who he really was, and why he'd come.

He caught a sight of the woman standing close to the shore, though he couldn't make out her features or see her hair under the rain slicker she wore. He'd see soon enough, he thought, and gently guided the plane lower.

Without warning, an explosion rocked the tail end of his plane and sent the machine into a downward tilt. Smoke filled the cockpit, and there was the choking stench of burning metal in the air. Guy swore hotly, and frantically struggled with the controls. But it was no good.

He was going down and there wasn't a damn thing he could do about it. Well, fate certainly did have a strange sense of humor. He'd come here to change Holly's life, and she was the only one who could now save his.

FORTUNES OF TEXAS: THE LOST HEIRS

Fortune Family Tree

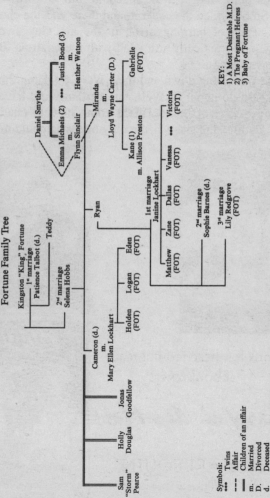

Kingston "King" Fortune

1st marriage — Patience Talbot (d.)
 └ Teddy

2nd marriage — Selena Hobbs

Daniel Smythe *** Emma Michaels (2) *** Justin Bond (3)
m. Heather Watson

Emma Michaels
m. Flynn Sinclair
 └ Miranda
   m. Lloyd Wayne Carter (D.)
    └ Gabrielle (FOT)

Kane (1)
m. Allison Preston
 └ Victoria (FOT)

Ryan

1st marriage — Janine Lockhart
 Matthew (FOT) Zane (FOT) Dallas (FOT) Vanessa (FOT)

2nd marriage — Sophie Barnes (d.)

3rd marriage — Lily Redgrove
 └ (FOT)

Cameron (d.)
m. Mary Ellen Lockhart
 Holden (FOT) Logan (FOT) Eden (FOT)

Jonas Goodfellow

Holly Douglas

Sam "Storm" Pearce

KEY:
1) A Most Desirable M.D.
2) The Pregnant Heiress
3) Baby of Fortune

Symbols:
*** Twins
- - - Affair
Children of an affair
m. Married
D. Divorced
d. Deceased
FOT Romance takes place in original
Fortunes of Texas 12 Book Continuity

If you enjoyed what you just read,
then we've got an offer you can't resist!

Take 2 bestselling
love stories FREE!

Plus get a FREE surprise gift!

**SILHOUETTE®
MAKES YOU
A STAR!**

Feel like a star with Silhouette.

We will fly you and a guest to New York City for an
exciting weekend stay at a glamorous 5-star hotel.
Experience a refreshing day at one of New York's
trendiest spas and have your photo taken by a
professional. Plus, receive $1,000 U.S. spending money!

Flowers...long walks...dinner for two...
how does Silhouette Books
make romance come alive for you?

Send us a script, with 500 words or less, along with visuals (only drawings,
magazine cutouts or photographs or combination thereof). Show us how
Silhouette Makes Your Love Come Alive. Be creative and have fun. No
purchase necessary. All entries must be clearly marked with your name,
address and telephone number. All entries will become property of
Silhouette and are not returnable. **Contest closes September 28, 2001.**

Please send your entry to: **Silhouette Makes You a Star!**

In U.S.A.	In Canada
P.O. Box 9069	P.O. Box 637
Buffalo, NY. 14269-9069	Fort Erie, ON, L2A 5X3

Look for contest details on the next page, by visiting www.eHarlequin.com or
request a copy by sending a self-addressed envelope to the applicable address
above. Contest open to Canadian and U.S. residents who are 18 or over.
Void where prohibited.

Silhouette®
Where love comes alive ™

Our lucky winner's photo will appear in a Silhouette ad. Join the fun!

SRMYAS1

HARLEQUIN "SILHOUETTE MAKES YOU A STAR!" CONTEST 1308
OFFICIAL RULES
NO PURCHASE NECESSARY TO ENTER

1. To enter, follow directions published in the offer to which you are responding. Contest begins June 1, 2001, and ends on September 28, 2001. Entries must be postmarked by September 28, 2001, and received by October 5, 2001. Enter by hand-printing (or typing) on an 8 ¹/₂" x 11" piece of paper your name, address (including zip code), contest number/name and attaching a script containing <u>500 words or less, <u>along with drawings, photographs or magazine cutouts, or combinations thereof</u> (i.e., collage) <u>on no larger than 9" x 12"</u> piece of paper, describing how the <u>Silhouette books make romance come alive for you.</u> Mail via first-class mail to: Harlequin "Silhouette Makes You a Star!" Contest 1308, (in the U.S.) P.O. Box 9069, Buffalo, NY 14269-9069, (in Canada) P.O. Box 637, Fort Erie, Ontario, Canada L2A 5X3. Limit one entry per person, household or organization.

2. Contests will be judged by a panel of members of the Harlequin editorial, marketing and public relations staff. Fifty percent of criteria will be judged against script and fifty percent will be judged against drawing, photographs and/or magazine cutouts. Judging criteria will be based on the following:

   - Sincerity—25%
   - Originality and Creativity—50%
   - Emotionally Compelling—25%

   In the event of a tie, duplicate prizes will be awarded. Decisions of the judges are final.

3. All entries become the property of Torstar Corp. and may be used for future promotional purposes. Entries will not be returned. No responsibility is assumed for lost, late, illegible, incomplete, inaccurate, nondelivered or misdirected mail.

4. Contest open only to residents of the U.S. <u>(except Puerto Rico)</u> and Canada who are 18 years of age or older, and is void wherever prohibited by law; all applicable laws and regulations apply. Any litigation within the Province of Quebec respecting the conduct or organization of a publicity contest may be submitted to the Régie des alcools, des courses et des jeux for a ruling. Any litigation respecting the awarding of a prize may be submitted to the Régie des alcools, des courses et des jeux only for the purpose of helping the parties reach a settlement. Employees and immediate family members of Torstar Corp. and D. L. Blair, Inc., their affiliates, subsidiaries and all other agencies, entities and persons connected with the use, marketing or conduct of this contest are not eligible to enter. Taxes on prizes are the sole responsibility of the winner. Acceptance of any prize offered constitutes permission to use winner's name, photograph or other likeness for the purposes of advertising, trade and promotion on behalf of Torstar Corp., its affiliates and subsidiaries without further compensation to the winner, unless prohibited by law.

5. Winner will be determined no later than November 30, 2001, and will be notified by mail. Winner will be required to sign and return an Affidavit of Eligibility/Release of Liability/Publicity Release form within 15 days after winner notification. Noncompliance within that time period may result in disqualification and an alternative winner may be selected. All travelers must execute a Release of Liability prior to ticketing and must possess required travel documents (e.g., passport, photo ID) where applicable. Trip must be booked by December 31, 2001, and completed within one year of notification. No substitution of prize permitted by winner. Torstar Corp. and D. L. Blair, Inc., their parents, affiliates and subsidiaries are not responsible for errors in printing of contest, entries and/or game pieces. In the event of printing or other errors that may result in unintended prize values or duplication of prizes, all affected game pieces or entries shall be null and void. **Purchase or acceptance of a product offer does not improve your chances of winning.**

6. Prizes: (1) Grand Prize—A 2-night/3-day trip for two (2) to New York City, including round-trip coach air transportation nearest winner's home and hotel accommodations (double occupancy) at The Plaza Hotel, a glamorous afternoon makeover at <u>a trendy New York spa</u>, $1,000 in U.S. spending money and an opportunity to <u>have a professional photo taken and appear in a Silhouette advertisement</u> (approximate retail value: $7,000). (10) Ten Runner-Up Prizes of gift packages (retail value $50 ea.). Prizes consist of only those items listed as part of the prize. Limit one prize per person. Prize is valued in U.S. currency.

7. For the name of the winner (available after December 31, 2001) send a self-addressed, stamped envelope to: Harlequin "Silhouette Makes You a Star!" Contest 1197 Winners, P.O. Box 4200 Blair, NE 68009-4200 or you may access the www.eHarlequin.com Web site through February 28, 2002.

Contest sponsored by Torstar Corp., P.O. Box 9042, Buffalo, NY 14269-9042.

SRMYAS2

COMING NEXT MONTH

#1387 THE MILLIONAIRE COMES HOME—Mary Lynn Baxter
Man of the Month
Millionaire Denton Hardesty returned to his hometown only to find himself face-to-face with Grace Simmons—the lover he'd never forgotten. Spending time at Grace's bed-and-breakfast, Denton realized he wanted to rekindle the romance he'd broken off years ago. Now all he had to do was convince Grace that *this* time he intended to stay…forever.

#1388 COMANCHE VOW—Sheri WhiteFeather
In keeping with the old Comanche ways, Nick Bluestone promised to marry his brother's widow, Elaina Myers-Bluestone, and help raise her daughter. Love wasn't supposed to be part of the bargain, but Nick couldn't deny the passion he found in Elaina's embrace. Could Nick risk his heart and claim Elaina as his wife...*in every way?*

#1389 WHEN JAYNE MET ERIK—Elizabeth Bevarly
20 Amber Court
That's me, bride-on-demand Jayne Pembroke, about to get hitched to the one and only drop-dead gorgeous Erik Randolph. The proposal was simple enough—one year together and we'd both get what we wanted. But one taste of those spine-tingling kisses and I was willing to bet things were going to get a whole lot more complicated!

#1390 FORTUNE'S SECRET DAUGHTER—Barbara McCauley
Fortunes of Texas: The Lost Heirs
When store owner Holly Douglas rescued injured bush pilot Guy Blackwolf after his plane crashed into a lake by her home, she found herself irresistibly attracted to the charming rogue and his magnetic kisses. But would she be able to entrust her heart to Guy once she learned the secret he had kept from her?

#1391 SLEEPING WITH THE SULTAN—Alexandra Sellers
Sons of the Desert: The Sultans
When powerful and attractive Sheikh Ashraf abducted actress Dana Morningstar aboard his luxury yacht, he claimed that he was desperately in love with her and wanted the chance to gain her love in return. Dana knew she shouldn't trust Ashraf—but could she resist his passionate kisses and tender seduction?

#1392 THE BRIDAL ARRANGEMENT—Cindy Gerard
Lee Savage had promised to marry and take care of Ellie Shiloh in accordance with her father's wishes. Lee soon became determined to show his innocent young bride the world she had always been protected from. But he hadn't counted on Ellie's strength and courage to show him a thing or two…about matters of the heart.